LAST
LINE
OF A
Goat Song

JONATHAN DOYLE

Wild Thorn Publishing

Wild Thorn Publishing
www.wildthornpublishing.com

First Paperback Edition: January 2018

Library of Congress Control Number: 2017917428

ISBN: 978-1-948223-00-3

Printed in the United States of America

To the women in my life:
Linda, Amy, and Laura.

1

Two of William's best friends had died that day. One was murdered in cold blood and the other simply expired. So he crawled from the solitude of his faded single apartment with its Spartan décor, its twin bed and square bedside lamp table and walked out into the night, into the courtyard of the dilapidated apartment complex he'd lived in for decades. Though drunk, he knew to avoid the drained, cracked pool and the murmuring tenants who thought him too strange or old or pathetic for actual eye contact and crawled under the only bush he found that was near to an open window. He carried with him what was left of the bottle of cheap whiskey in one hand and a journal with a pen in the other.

As he sat in the dirt, his chin rested on his chest. The leather journal was in his lap with a pen attached to the side, as if the journal was a student's notebook. A typed letter, folded in half, was slipped in the middle of the journal. The bottle of whiskey was next to him. His eyes were watery and red, staring defiantly straight into the ether of the evening, focused on nothing.

He looked older than he needed to. He was sixty but could have been eighty on this night. His jeans sagged and his sweatshirt was faded and stained with an unknown condiment along the cuffs. He wore frailty like a winter shawl. He was searching for a sound to break the silence.

In the Los Angeles sky, high above the apartment courtyard where he hid in the bushes, dueling spotlights shone bright as they oscillated against the hills of Hollywood and the rest of the city. William could see the careening circles of white through the branches. Below the lights, he knew important things were happening. Carpets were rolled out. Cameras were flashing. Quotes were jotted down. William had never been around the important things. He'd never walked on red carpets. The gold women in silk and short men in tall clothes had never been anywhere near William. He'd never been close enough to spotlights to get a good look. The lights in the sky seemed too large to him, too big and too far away to touch, but he watched them anyway, with a vacant stare. He took a swig of the whiskey, moving as few muscles as necessary to do so.

He waited for sound under the window and counted the times the lights in the sky crossed his sight path. After he had lost count near fifty, he wondered if the people inside the apartment building would ever speak. He knew they were home, he'd seen the lights flicker on from inside his own apartment a few doors down. He'd left his apartment and crawled under the bushes to find his seat beneath the windowpane. He needed to hear voices, so he had to wait.

He took another drink of the whiskey and was happy with the placid result. He blinked his eyes. He could feel the cracks in the corners of his lips. A cell phone rang from inside the apartment and he hoped that the person inside would answer it. At the very least he would hear one half of a conversation. But the phone rang until it didn't ring anymore and that was all. The television was flipped on. A woman with a blond voice calmly recited sterile words: "In Guatemala, a fire at a manufacturing plant killed twenty-nine factory workers in what some locals are calling the worst fatal workplace incident in the history of the small nation. A spokesperson for the Steamwell Corporation, which owns the plant, as well as such entities as Sire Foods Grocery and Captain Calrod's Footwear and Rifle, said the fire was a horrible accident, but wasn't due to any negligence on the part of the Corporation...." William hated the sound of the television. He wasn't interested in scripted words. They weren't real.

He decided to leave his camp. He scooted his way back under the bush, bottle and journal in hand, until he emerged onto the concrete path that cut a swath through the tendrils of the apartment complex.

William skulked along the path, searching for another open window to crouch beneath. Most were shut tight as the night was a bit too cool. He'd been doing this for so long, decades, hiding under windows, stealing conversations, that it had long ago quit seeming like aberrant behavior. He had moments of guilt about it, the constant spying and interloping. But those moments passed quickly now. He felt worse when he opened his old journal and wrote down the conversations he'd overheard, the phrases and speeches, word for word. He did this not because of thievery. He did it for those times when the loneliness got too hard to bear, when his sleep wouldn't come, when the whiskey didn't work and the lights in the sky, jaundiced and eternal, didn't shine the way they had promised him in dark theaters and church steeples. In those moments, usually at night, he needed to hear the tinny jolt of speech to calm him. But when the windows were all closed, the phones unanswered and the televisions muted, the resulting silence was too much for him to breathe through.

He'd then open his journal and read the pilfered conversations from the past. He'd recall the fluent syllables strung together so easily and masterfully. He'd read the words and fool himself into thinking that they were spoken to him or with him in mind or because of some great deed or action he'd accomplished. He did it to feel as though he had someone to talk to.

Tonight, a night when he'd seen the death of his two closest friends, his only two friends, he needed voices more than ever. He'd tried in vain to make his own voice work. But his voice was broken. He had an easy disease, a childhood stutter that calcified and expanded as he aged. That damn easy disease that locked his voice, frustrating everything he did, that was the impetus to a life full of silent nods and plastic loves. That fucking easy disease that rendered him immobile, useless, made his mind work so hard to do the seemingly simplest tasks – buying groceries, calling a family member, telling a woman that he loved her – impossible feats. Talk. William couldn't talk. Every other man or woman with a stutter outgrows it or overcomes it or learns to spit out a few words every once in a while. But not William. He never uttered a word. He was only able to dispense guttural moans and half-chewed, self-directed epithets.

He knew it wouldn't work, his voice, but he attempted to speak every day, out of habit. And when it didn't work, when the voice inside his head materialized as dry, arid coughs of muteness, he felt it was okay that he listened to and stole the voices from others. When he did that, when he wrote down what the others said through their windows, he thought it poetry, their banal conversations akin to the most glorious art. And when he read over his journal, when he remembered the words, the intonations, the sarcasm or irony, the exacerbation or humor, he smiled in the darkness and felt like one of those important people under the bright lights who walked upon the red carpets.

He blinked his eyes and felt the sting of rising tears. Still no sound came from the window and in its empty, silent place he had no choice but to remember.

The first death was his African grey parrot, a stubborn chanteuse who woke William up with a simple imperative: *Wake Up*. The bird repeated this phrase over and over with her husky timbre. She'd been gifted to William by his mother on his thirtieth birthday decades earlier. It was the perfect gift to give the isolated and wordless. The bird, named Sammy, had a voice, high pitched and atonal, which William loved. Sammy had personality. She cocked her head more like a Spaniel and learned to temper William's moods with the often humorous timing of her favorite phrase. *Wake up*, she sang.

His mother taught the bird to act as an alarm and companion for her youngest son. It was a good gift. For thirty years, when William walked through the neighborhood of his Hollywood home, when he faced canvassers selling him the trendy cause of the moment or children on bicycles, when he encountered the friendly banter of fellow pedestrians and service workers, each question that was posited in his direction acted like verbal shrapnel that he would later have to dig out and soothe over with long baths in lavender oil. But he knew his bird Sammy would be on her wooden perch in her silver cage, waiting patiently for William to open its door and stroke her feathers as the bird ran up and down William's finger. *Wake up*, she would say bluntly.

Sammy died. It just happened. She wasn't sick. Nothing strange happened the day before. Sammy ate her feed with her usual vigor. Still, William had woken up and the bird was dead. He'd stared at the dead bird for an hour before he took Sammy out of her cage and placed the body in an old shoebox and buried it under a tree on a grassy slope in the back of the apartment complex. Thus began a day that should have been normal, a day marked with nothing but mundane chores, a completed crossword, a shopping excursion, reading a book detailing the events leading up to the assassination of William McKinley, something William had been looking forward to starting. But with Sammy dying decades before she was supposed to, the day hadn't gone according to plan.

Dazed by the impromptu funeral, William went for a long walk. He paced up and down Fountain Avenue, passed the Burger Barn where he stole packets of ketchup, past the tenor of the troubadour on the corner, past the new buildings and repaved streets. He felt small and smaller as he paced, he floated more than walked. He wondered about god the way children did, in black-or-white tantrums, in all-or-nothing grandeur, angrily. He missed his bird from the very second he found her lifeless body. He was heartbroken. He had never asked for much and because of that, he felt his bird should have lived years longer. He wondered if he should get a new bird. But who would teach the bird to speak? His mother had been dead for twenty years. He knew no one else. And how do you replace something you love? Why do so many people want to replace love? So he paced and he thought.

He walked from Normandie to Cahuenga, to and fro like Sammy had done on her perch, looking through the silver slats of her cage at the room, the simple bed, the flickering computer on the small desk, the biographies of presidents that filled William's bookshelf. Now it was William who was looking through his cage at the strip malls and the layers of exhausted cars too tired to move, at the blue sky and felt the temperate air, until he finally came upon the centerpiece of the neighborhood, the mighty Sire Foods Inc., a sturdy monument to everything a person ever needed. William passed the mega store. He resisted its amenities, its countless corporate charms and continued mourning in the form of a pace. Finally, he went home and looked at that cage that he'd taken pristine care of for thirty years and he sat down on his bed and cried. William hadn't cried in a very long time and just as tragic, he couldn't remember why.

The second death would come just three hours later, at Sire Foods Inc., where his other friend worked. When William thought about it now, sitting under the window, the smell of juniper in his nose, he thought of standing at the edge of a bay, watching the water lap benignly against the rocks of the jetty, feeling the hard sand of the shore under his feet and squinting his eyes towards the horizon where row boats floated, lovers inside, hand-holding atop the current just a few seconds before the water pulled back from the shore and turned violent and tidal.

His eyes blinked again in the darkness. He took another drink.

The second window that he hid under didn't remain silent. The voices hit William and he smiled. That was what he wanted. Another swig of whiskey, those spotlights still bouncing off the dark blue sky.

"I can't live here much longer," the male voice said. William knew the man who was speaking, he'd seen him walking from his car to his front door, hair cut close to his scalp, carrying takeout food of various ethnicities, wearing the boring attire of an ageless person, beige pants and a button down shirt, never giving away if he was too old or too young.

"What are you talking about? We moved here together," the female voice questioned. William thought her voice was too much sometimes, too strong. It seemed to need to be more than a collection of syllables, as if she was ashamed of her Nashville twang when William would have coveted it.

"It's so crowded, hon."

William loved the word *hon*. It felt colloquial and private and there was no way to say the word *hon* without it coming across warm and ingratiating. Even when it was used condescendingly, it still had innate charm. He wrote down that word in his journal and underlined it three times.

"It's Los Angeles. You have a great job."

"I answer phones."

"Baby steps."

"But what are we stepping towards?"

A pause in the conversation. William pictured the female with her pixie cut and red lips, loose dress flowing, the generic floral print twirled by her own hand, slinking towards him, her boyfriend, and intertwining her fingers in his, marrying them as he sat in the kitchen trying to pay attention to the game.

"We came here for a reason," she said. William wondered what the reason was.

"I know. I just wonder why we can't move to Venice if we have to stay here. I told you I would give it a year. It's been two."

"Venice is too far for my auditions. Anything can happen here. And you love it here."

"You don't really believe that. Sometimes I do. Sometimes I just want to see more white people," he said. Her laugh sounded tight and nervous and so did his. They stopped talking. William scooted along the dirt until he once again was at the foot of the concrete walk. He rose up with his belongings and ambled down the path. He stopped at Apartment 7, Maggie's apartment. Her light was on. She had come home. He looked in all directions, the coast was clear. He slipped yet again under the bushes. He had been under Maggie's window so many times a pathway had formed from where his body had repeatedly wriggled its way through the brush. The thicket no longer scratched him as he pushed through.

Once under her window, with the bottle between his legs and journal in his left hand, he again felt oddly satiated. From his pocket, he took out a small wooden rabbit's foot. He studied it. It was a simple child's toy. He shouldn't have possession of it. It belonged to Pedro, his friend who worked at Sire Foods, Inc.

Maggie had just come home from work. She was drinking something. William heard the ice clink in her glass. He hadn't heard Monster but he may have been there, in the shower, in the back room, getting ready for the night.

William closed his eyes and drank from the bottle. He gripped the wooden rabbit's foot and then put it back in his pocket. *Fuck. Fuck.* If only Sammy hadn't died, he would have followed his normal pattern. For a man who doesn't speak, the pattern is everything. The grid, the matrix, the order. After he'd paced, after he'd cried, he decided to salvage as much of his pattern as he could. He would go to Sire Foods, as he always did on Tuesdays, to see Pedro and pick up his groceries. But this time Pedro would see the sorrow in his eyes, the residual weariness from the death of his bird, and ask him what was wrong. William would shake his head and Pedro would understand that whatever happened was grave and heavy. Pedro would speak in low tones, in eulogy. William would find some comfort there in one of the endless aisles of Sire Foods.

So, he did. He rushed down Fountain to get there before Pedro's shift was over. On his way there, a canvasser asked him to donate his signature to the dying fisheries. He avoided the woman by adopting his look of insanity. Crazy eyes, he had named it. It worked. She left him alone but it still cost him valuable minutes. If Pedro didn't help him, if he'd already left for the day, he'd have to gather the groceries himself then wait in line, then the cashier would speak to him. For a man that didn't talk, this was too much. They would look at him like his easy disease was contagious.

In the store, he searched for Pedro but couldn't find him. It was so much later than when William usually shopped. If only he'd come at his normal time. But he hadn't. If only Sammy hadn't died and the canvasser hadn't warned him about the fading salmon and the fading tuna. If only he walked on the red carpets. If only Sire Foods delivered. If only he wasn't all alone. If only he could speak.

William showed up just a few minutes too late.

William didn't want to remember anymore. He brushed the dirt and fallen leaves from the bushes into little piles like a schoolboy.

Then, finally, he heard her. Maggie was singing, which meant Monster wasn't with her. She only sang when she was alone. She didn't have a great voice but she had a committed voice. The pitch was sharp, sometimes flat, but never shaky. Tonight, she sang in Spanish. A folk song. The song was the story of a boy who dreamed of owning the sky, then owned the sky and painted it blue to impress the girl who wasn't impressed at all. So the boy who owned the sky cried and rain was formed.

Sometimes, when William sat with his back against her wall, under the window, listening to Maggie live her life, he could sense that she was on the other side of the wall with her back to his, knees up into her chest, secretly happy someone was listening to her sing.

The lights in the sky had stopped. The movie was apparently over. The vices that trapped the city were just taking hold. Los Angeles was holding its breath. William crawled out of the bushes as he had done so many times before. But instead of finding a new window to covet or finally going back to his empty apartment, he walked to Maggie's door. The woman whom he'd been listening to, protecting, watching over for fifteen years, the woman he'd passed in the courtyard as a stranger countless times. The woman who had no idea how much he knew about her, that he knew everything about her, that she was the closest thing he'd ever had to a child. She didn't know him. She didn't know that two deaths on the same day had made him desperate to feel movement, to find wind on his face, to upend sixty years of shadow lurking and being burned by the sun. William didn't want to do what he was about to do. He was petrified. But he was compelled to act by some greater force, by a god or a devil, or maybe guilt, surely guilt, and by a feral desire to scream and yell and be heard.

As he approached her door, he took out the letter he'd written earlier that night. He lifted it towards the sky and said a few silent words to Sammy and Pedro. Then, with all the calmness he could muster, though his hands still shook with tredpidation, he rapped on the door of his neighbor, who was still singing the little Mexican folk song she'd learned as a child.

2

William waited in his apartment for two hours with his bags packed. He had rifled through his suitcases twenty five times to make sure he'd packed everything he needed. Though, he told himself before unzipping the bag for the twenty-sixth time, he really had no idea what *everything* meant in this case. He had never left Los Angeles, save for that one time to go to Palm Springs to visit his father who had relocated there in the late 70s to cure his arthritis. There was a very good chance he had no idea what he needed. His hand rested on the zipper, pushing it back and forth along its teeth. William liked Palm Springs. He remembered the rocks and the dryness. He always told himself he would go back one day.

He finally decided he had looked through his luggage enough and laid the handle of his bag against the door and went and sat on the small chair by the empty birdcage. He peered in, looking for a ghost, for molted feathers and droppings, examining the eroded tread of the perch where Sammy liked to stand the most. If Sammy had lived, William thought, he wouldn't be leaving. His fingers, still needing something to do, played the silver cell like a harp.

William made sure the gas was off. He checked the circuit box, turned off the water, locked all the windows and bolted shut the back door through the kitchen. As he did these things, the weight of what he was about to embark on hit him and he started breathing heavy. He felt the small wooden rabbit's foot in his pocket and it was heavy like the cross. He could just leave it on the counter and not do this. This was insanity, it wasn't the sort of thing he did. This didn't make any sense. He was a man of simple routines. He went into his cupboard and pulled out a bottle of Irish whiskey. The good stuff. He did two long pulls on it. It burned but he didn't flinch. He didn't have to do this, the whiskey told him – the way whiskey tends to. He shook his head and checked his bag one last time.

He heard her coming up the path to her apartment and he took a deep breath. She slammed her front door and he took that as his cue to wait for her outside. He grabbed his bag and turned around at the front door, looking back onto his little home on Fountain where he had lived for 27 years. A week, he told himself. I'll be back in a week. Maybe two weeks. He could return to all of this. Maybe he would get a new bird. Maybe he could ask Maggie to teach it a new phrase. Then he tipped a hat he wasn't wearing to the empty space and walked out into the mild evening air.

She came out a half an hour later with two suitcases compared to his one. He tried to hide his slight shiver. She saw him look at her pile of stuff.

"I'm a girl. Cut me some slack."

He smiled.

She wore a hoodie and loose fitting jeans and he thought she looked perfect for a road trip. He followed her out back, picking up one of the bags that fell from her grip.

The midnight blue van was in his parking space. He had spent considerable time washing it that morning and it almost glowed in the dusk. A stencil of a large bouquet of brightly hued flowers dominated each side. Above each stencil the simple words "HAPPY FLOWERS" arced like a rainbow. She opened the back doors so he could load in the bags. She watched him feebly try and lift her bags, rolled her eyes, then scooped them up and half-tossed them into the back.

"I have to throw out drunks all the time. Builds upper body strength." He nodded and smelled his breath discreetly, afraid it might reek. With the trunk closed, the two stood there looking at the ground.

"Well, I guess we should go. I guess we should do this. We should do this, right?"

He looked up and their eyes met. He tried to open his mouth to speak, but quickly reached his hand up and forced his lips shut. Then he smirked. The brown of his eyes lit up under the reverse halo of a streetlamp.

He nodded. She nodded, too.

Maggie got comfortable behind the wheel. She started the engine and put it in reverse. The van smelled like pine and cigarettes, evoking William's memories of the burning embers of his father's Pall Malls hanging off of his fingertips, black snakes near his yellow fingers. As a kid, he would watch with wonder as the snake coiled down, his father lost in thought and unaware of the expanding creature of ash.

Maggie fiddled with the mirrors and put on the air conditioning. He fiddled with the window, used the roller to roll it up, down. His legs shook rapidly. Once out of the parking spot, she began to accelerate forward and then she stopped, slamming on the brakes.

"Listen, I don't know why I'm doing this, other than I got shitfaced and started feeling bad for things I can't control and for one fleeting moment thought this was the right thing to do. I don't really know who you are but let's just agree that we're here to help each other. You're giving my family this van and I'm taking you where you need to go. It's a brief marriage of convenience. I know you don't speak, which is really fucking bizarre, but whatever, we all have our things."

Maggie twirled the string of her hoodie around her finger, round and round. "A few rules. First, no shaking."

William put his hands on his legs and forced them to stop. He smiled sheepishly.

"Second, no touching me."

She let the string unravel from her finger.

"I know you're a decent man but you're still a man. Don't lay a hand on me. There, I said it. It's out there, it's been dealt with. We can move on from it. The elephant's been slain. Third, you know, let's just try and make this as pleasant a trip as possible. I've got some good music and we have this van, which seems to be in decent shape, if a bit tacky. Hopefully it'll be sunny and bright and we'll just have a really good time together. Maybe we can have some sort of *Oprah* moment and learn from each other's differences. I think I took a college course on situations just like this. Well, I never went to college, but I saw it on *Friends*, maybe. At any rate, let's just do our best to enjoy the strangeness." She paused. "Because I won't be enjoying a thing once we get to where we're going."

William wanted to comfort her and tell her that he didn't really know why he was doing this, either. Instead, he focused hard on keeping his legs still. She pushed the gas pedal down and the two of them were heading south towards Mexico.

3

———

They drove through the alley behind the apartment complex. William felt a twinge of panic as Maggie turned onto Cole Avenue. William had lived on this block, in these apartments, his entire life. He hadn't given that much thought, the issue of permanence, until he recognized that it was fleeing from him. For the first time, he was heading in the opposite direction of every place that he knew. He wanted to say goodbye or thank you. But he said nothing, as was his custom. Maggie, unaware of William's anxiety, sped the car forward.

At the next light, Maggie turned on the blinker and waited to turn left. From the passenger side window of his late father's relic of a van, William saw his life as a pastiche. The neighborhood, sometimes Hollywood, sometimes Los Angeles, sometimes just east or west of somewhere else, had changed from glamorous to suburban to decayed to livable, from white to brown to gay to Russian and now some other eclectic mix. Blinks of an eye at the unfettered America.

On the corner, where the van waited for the light to change, was an industrial unit, run down and no longer in use, that had once been the elementary school that William had attended as a child. William squinted to find the shape of the old school building within the new building, a palimpsest in his memory. He could see it, square and brown, the flagpole in the middle, lurking just beneath what stood now. He could see the black parking lot hiding behind it and the long-forgotten cars parked there, their thick metal giving them an idle sheen. He remembered one of his teachers with her blond bun swept up like a golden conch shell, as she watched from the edge of the small playground as the other kids ran and yelled and laughed. He could just make out his young self, seven, maybe eight, peering from the window inside his classroom, within the blunt building, always looking outside at the kids and the conch-haired teacher. He would listen to their yells and cheers with his hands jammed deep in his pockets, his brown eyes reflecting in the window, and sometimes his breath, too, staining the glass over and over, as his mind wavered between wanting to join the others and praying to see his mother's Ford turning the corner to pick him up. Maybe if he'd gone out to that playground, he would have outgrown the stammer and the stutter. But he didn't. As a little boy, William stayed looking through the classroom window. Maybe he had never really outgrown being that little boy. Maybe he was stuck there, like some volcanic freeze frame, feeling an ever-present twinge of malarial nostalgia.

"William, I have to stop at the bar I work at real quick. Cool?" Maggie asked.

William nodded.

The light changed and the van turned left. William let the school and what had become of the school fall behind as the asphalt urged them forward.

She pulled the van into the parking lot in front of the bar, which didn't seem to have a name. Just a door with a green *open* sign above it.

"I shouldn't be long. If you want to run and get something to drink or snack on, there's a liquor store on the corner," Maggie said, pointing to Louie's Liquor, which was lit up like Christmas.

Maggie slammed the car door and jogged towards the bar. William sat in the car and counted his breaths, trying to decide if he should stay in the van or venture out across the asphalt.

The second Maggie was inside the bar, she leaned up against the wall and closed her eyes.

"What the fuck am I doing?" she said to no one. The bar was empty. Her eyes flew open and she studied the emptiness of the room, which never failed to feel strange and off and slightly frightening. She liked the bar when it was full, when the people who inhabited it were busy chiseling their habits, when the men flirted with her and gave her paternal advice as they imbibed, told her college, marriage, motherhood were all right or all wrong. The barflies that she'd come to know and love, drunken rabbles of porous men, had come to mean something more to Maggie than just a tip and an ego boost. There was a permanence attached to them. These men were like old photographs hung crooked on a family room wall display. They were a home of her choosing. And the bar felt skeletal without them. They were the missing tendons that connected everything.

She went to the register and took out a few hundred dollars in cash. She wrote a quick note, an IOU for her uncle, who owned the bar. She looked around again, then dug for something in her pocket, a piece of paper. She unfolded it and read it:

I come to you in the night with an odd request. I know that I am a stranger to you. An old man you walk past from time to time, a person who happens to share a wall with you. Well, I am in debt to a very great man and it seems it is now time for me to repay my debt. You see, this man was very kind to me. Has anyone ever been truly kind to you? I would imagine your father bought you dollhouses as a child or your mother took you for ice cream. Maybe a boyfriend gave you flowers and chocolates. Pardon me if these examples seem old fashioned. They are, and I guess I am, too. Well, in any event, perhaps I could fill that spot of kindness for you. You see, I inadvertently overheard you talk with your uncle (I presume) not that long ago about your family's need for a van. Maggie, I would like to provide you with a van. I will happily give away my family's van, one that I don't use, as I don't drive, to your family. (Well, I do drive, but my license has long been expired and I prefer to walk.) It would mean so much to me to be able to help in this small way. I must, however, ask for one small favor in return for the van. I need a ride. To Mexico. To the town of La Ciudad de Martine, which I believe is somewhere in the middle of the country. It is the only way that I can repay my debt to the man. You give me a ride down to where I need to go, plus a ride to the airport after we are finished with my errand, and I will happily give your family ownership of my vehicle.

I hope you don't find this offer too forward or too strange, and, yes, I realize it is certainly both of those very things, but I must know your answer to this out-of-the-blue request. Know that all of us, until such time as we meet, are strangers.

William Thornton

Maggie found the whole thing bizarre. She fished her phone out of her pocket and put the note away.

"Lupe, it's me. I'm doing this. This old man knocks on my door, gives me a note and twenty-four hours later I'm in a van with him."

"Read the note to me again," Lupe said.

Maggie did. As she read the note, she heard the sounds of San Francisco in the background, the shuffling, cracked renegades of the Tenderloin homeless, the trolley chimes echoing down Market, the liberalness of a certain kind of freedom. She was saying William's words, but she was thinking of Lupe and Ernesto, her cousin and her cousin's husband, who'd met a year prior and married seven months ago, packing up an old Ford Taurus and driving it to the Bay Area on a sunny day in the middle of a sunny week for some version of a new life. Maggie and Monster stood in the street as the sedan pulled away and disappeared. Monster, in his Lakers sweats and loose wife beater, pulled Maggie close to him and whispered in her ear that he wanted to break open an eight ball and fuck all night. Maggie let him tongue her ear. She waved after the car as it eclipsed the horizon.

She wanted to leave with Lupe. Crawl in the back of the sedan and surprise her somewhere near Fresno. Her skin itched from where Monster touched it but it was a false itch. Every day after Lupe had left, Maggie told herself that she would go see her cousin in the Bay Area, take the 5 as far north as Oakland. Ride the Bart into the City and get lost in the hills and the homeless. She would get swallowed up in a quake and lose herself to the drugs south of Market, she would fly off Twin Peaks and take a dive from the bridge. But she never went.

The sedan finally turned the corner and Monster begged her with little boy humor to follow him into the apartment so they could begin to snort and fuck. She followed him inside, like she always did.

Maggie finished reading William's letter.

"And he's definitely giving you a van?"

"I drove it to the bar."

"And you told Tío everything?"

"I told him. He thinks it's a sign from heaven. He thinks Mama's prayers have been working and this is the answer. I just have to be back in two weeks for work. God isn't quite powerful enough to get any more of my shifts covered."

"And do we think this guy is gonna rape you or something?"

"Lupe, you've seen him. He's harmless. A piece of gum stuck on the ground. And I think he and I sort of covered that already. It's just so strange."

Lupe must have been climbing a hill. Her voice began to find heaviness.

"Are you ready to see her?"

"Mama? Of course not."

"She's not that bad," Lupe said. "I always loved her. I always thought she was something to behold. She made me think of Mary."

"I wish you were coming with me. I could do this with you. Come and drive the van to Mexico so she can have it to sell her crops or whatever she needs it for."

Lupe let Maggie spin. She waited for a free moment.

"I meant are you ready to see Jessica?"

The name stung Maggie through the phone.

"I know what you meant. Tío's been trying to get me to go home for fifteen years, so has Mama."

"So why are you doing it?"

"I'm thirty. I guess it's time. And, no, I'm not ready."

Lupe told her she loved her and that she missed her and that she wanted to see her soon. Maggie said something similar back to her.

I could be going to San Francisco on vacation, Maggie thought as she texted Monster that she was stopping by to see him. Then she texted her uncle to tell him she picked up spending money and that the van was in good condition, that Mama would approve. Or, she thought, I could do what I'm doing instead: take the 5 South, past San Diego and Tijuana, with ubiquitous plumes of smog that make LA look clear as Alaska, dig deep into Mexico, somewhere in the middle, somewhere that doesn't count anywhere but there, forgotten to the world at large and be with her family. A falsely excited "Hello!" to her daughter and a big bear hug that won't be reciprocated – that will be rejected. Maggie will kiss her mother's fat, round, sun-ruined cheek and elicit growls from one of her brothers. She'd dance the way the bad girls tended to dance, in perfect rhythm, when the night of the party came (as it always did). She'd do it all without even trying, the dancing and the dying, without tequila, without meaning to. She'd dance and die the way bad girls have been dancing and dying since time began: By the general reproach of those who love them most.

She waited for the return texts to come through. Both the men in her life responded the same way: *K*.

4

William walked around the small liquor store looking at the sheen of the bottles and the glare of the packaged food. He could see dust on the top of canned soups and fading orange stickers with dollar amounts stuck to the sides of boxes of macaroni and cheese. The man behind the counter wore a turban and was watching a television show. William couldn't see what show was airing. The man was chewing gum and was engrossed in the program. William felt something rub up against his leg. It was a grey-and-white cat. William bent down to pet the cat but the cat ran away. It peered at William from the end of the aisle. William stared back. He wanted to call the cat to come back, like he had wanted to call out to Pedro before they shot him, the men in the masks. The fluorescent light of the liquor store burned into the air like the fluorescent lights at Sire Foods, Inc.

"Can I ged for you someding?" The man in the turban asked.

Peaches and whiskey, William thought. That's what he would have purchased from Pedro at Sire Foods. But Pedro would have known. Pedro knew that on Tuesdays William bought peaches, whiskey, bird food, tomatoes and rice. Every Tuesday it was the same.

The man behind the counter asked him the question again. The man seemed annoyed or maybe alarmed. William nodded, as if that could substitute for words. He grabbed a Coke and a candy bar and paid the man.

As he walked out into the early afternoon, Maggie was walking back from the bar. She seemed rushed, maybe even panicked. William wanted to reassure, but he didn't know how. He opened his Coke and offered it to her.

"No thanks, William. But we better get going."

As the car raced down the 110, going deeper into South Central, the high, looming concrete levees turned the freeway into a concrete river. William was having second thoughts. He eyed the lock on the door. He felt the grip of the door handle and tugged on it gently. The music was a man wailing out pedestrian complaints and William hated it. It was one thing to hear her singing along with it in the morning through the wall, but in the van, where he couldn't escape it? It lacked melody. It lacked story. It was a sonic rupture. Plus, it wasn't Maggie singing. Nervous, his legs began to shake again.

"I said no shaking." Maggie said.

William stopped them. He rubbed the wooden rabbit's foot in his pocket and closed his eyes and wished he had bought whiskey.

He found himself not wanting to look at Maggie. After all those years of window grazing, it was awkward for him to be sitting next to her. The proportion was off, a boy in his father's suit. He looked at the cars for soothing and was struck with a child's awe at the fever pitch of action in the world outside the van that encapsulated him. How could so many people be going so many places? And where were they all going? He had needed to witness a murder to get him on this freeway. William was hypnotized by this thought, by the casual lane change of the tan Volvo with the Greenpeace sticker on its bumper, by the disengaged stare of the woman in the Camry driving eighty and sipping a Diet Coke, by the movement, the endless stream of ravaged energy churning down these astral tunnels. And when his next patch of nerves tried to overtake him, he answered them with a strong resolve, with a thundering, guttural meta-voice: *Look at all I've missed because of you.*

Maggie tried not to look over at him. His lips were moving, twitching. If she thought too much about anything she knew that she would stop the car and turn around. She could be back in her room, legs up on her pink princess bed, smoking a joint, staring at the masculine green walls, listening to Morrissey bemoan everything. She could be going in the opposite direction of the garish land of ponchos and mariachis, the land where her mother ruled and her daughter lurked.

"I have to make a quick stop in Long Beach. You mind? I thought maybe that we could grab some dinner. Then we can hightail it to San Diego and find a motel for the night."

William nodded. He wondered if Long Beach was anything like Palm Springs.

5

She pulled off the 710 and started winding through street after street, one following the other. William eyed Maggie curiously, looking for a sign of danger or befuddlement but none came. She seemed focused and steady, even miming the words to the noise on the radio from time to time. So, he turned and looked out the window, watching the new city pass before him, a litany of convenience stores and grooming shops and apartment complexes with names like The West Elm and Pacific Winds. Finally, Maggie stopped in front of a house and pulled into its driveway.

"Listen, I have to run in and see some friends for a minute. Wait here."

William watched her go. The house was filled with people. She opened the front door without knocking and disappeared from William's view. William wondered what drug she was going to get. He knew she had a cocaine habit. He had often listened to her and Lupe talk late into the night about childhood or taking over the world, and still be at it when he awoke the next morning. He missed hearing Lupe. He missed hearing Lupe and Maggie together. He felt paternal towards both of the girls. He remembered when they first arrived, their uncle barking orders and directing the young girls on where to sit and where not to sit. They were wet rags then. Maggie stood out, with small unsure eyes excavating the scenes, looking for escape routes, rummaging through the rooms and hallways of her new home. Lupe hardly did anything. The girls often huddled together in the middle of a small bed, two strays, flecks of English delivered in soft, teenaged sprays. He cried for them, for their fears, real and imagined. Lupe was afraid of school. She was afraid of work. She was afraid of movement. Maggie calmed her, she took the first steps and reached back to guide Lupe through. All of this, William heard from his unseen window perch. He was proud when Maggie understood the first of her verb changes, when she solved an irregular conjugation, when she used "I am all right" instead of "I be all right." It wasn't long before Maggie outlawed Spanish so that Lupe might master English. Soon the girls were laughing and espousing the attractiveness of this movie star or that. They danced ballet hip-hop, took up the guitar. Their accents waned. They watched movie after movie, late night talk shows and daytime nonsense. William was intoxicated by the daring of it all, these girls from a distant land conquering Los Angeles.

Soon boys came over in place of the vacated uncle and the accent of immigrant girls evolved to something more native than foreign. He left when the boys turned to men and began to spend the night, but William was always on guard, a vigilant, silent protector of the young women.

After Lupe moved, he was even more vigilant. Maggie did more drugs than she had with Lupe. Maggie would try and be brave when calling her old home in Mexico, talking to her mother or sister, telling her family that Lupe had found love and taken a chance on it and that chance took her to San Francisco with her new husband. But William knew better. He knew Maggie was devastated by Lupe's departure and he knew Maggie kept things from her family. Her voice changed. Even in Spanish, which he understood fluently, he could hear the difference in tone between family and friend. It quivered, the long vowel sounds twisted like minor tempests. *Families can be difficult*, William wanted to tell her.

He watched as Maggie headed into the party and knew she'd come out a different person.

When a few minutes turned into a half an hour, William began to worry. He didn't want to leave the car but he began to wonder if Maggie was okay. He had been a high school janitor. He knew drug people. They had a smell to them, a certain scent of something not quite right, wet incense or rusted pine, and he felt a rush to find her and keep her safe from those types of men. He decided to take a look around, navigate the perimeter, make sure Maggie was okay.

He crept casually along the side of the house. No one was there. When he reached the backyard, a few partygoers were smoking and talking in and around a hammock that hung from two avocado trees. William stayed in the dark along the edge of the driveway. He looked in through the kitchen window and spotted Maggie conversing and joking with a group of young people. William assumed Monster was in there somewhere but couldn't see him.

He watched her for a moment. She was laughing, sipping a beer. She seemed so happy. William rarely saw her happy. He wished that moment could be extrapolated and placed in celluloid so that she might replay it over and over through his strained vision. If only she could see what he saw. Maggie moved away from the window's view, off into the labyrinth of the revelry. She was fine, William thought. He had worried over nothing.

He took another step down the drive and stumbled across an ice chest. He opened it and took two beers. Emboldened, he kept walking until he found the garage. He went in through the side door and shut it quickly, looking back to make sure he hadn't been seen. When he was sure he was alone, he looked around the garage. It had been converted into a den of sorts.

William took a seat on the stained, ripped sofa that stood like a tired bull in the corner. He watched the front door and waited anxiously for it to open, for young people to come crashing in, tensed at the thought.

The room was a mish mash of tools, posters, relics, trash. He began to feel sick.

This wasn't Palm Springs, he wasn't with his father. Somehow, he had developed into an old man, older than his father had ever become.

He rushed out through the side door and threw up over the dead roses that lined the garage. He coughed and choked out the refuse. He hadn't vomited in a very long time and forgot the pain it induced, the fear of too many breathless moments. He sucked in air after it was over and wiped his mouth clean with his jacket. In the window of a back room, Monster and Maggie reappeared. Why he was called Monster, William didn't know. He was tall, but thin and wore a sparse goatee on his pointed chin. They were talking close to each other, most likely arguing. They left the room, Maggie first, Monster chasing.

William tried to follow them as their images passed through the small square windows that ran down the hallway. He scurried down the drive, chasing the floating visages.

"Did you just throw up? You poor thing," a young woman said, obscured by the dark.

William froze and then turned to look at who had spoken to him. He could barely make out the image of a body. Then he turned back to see if he could find where Maggie and Monster had gone.

"When I drink too much, I make myself throw up. It just helps. Even if it's sort of gross," she said, uninterested by the fact that William seemed uninterested in her. She stepped into the illuminated halo made possible by a heat-activated flood light.

William nodded. She was attractive because she was young, maybe twenty-five.

"You're like a grandpa. That's cute."

Maggie and Monster were in the back bedroom. Monster was finger pointing in Maggie's direction. William walked towards them as if the walls of the house didn't stand between them. He moved down the driveway. Monster's finger hit Maggie above her left breast. The woman who called him grandpa followed close behind. William was beginning to feel nervous. The woman was too close to him.

"Are you gonna throw up again?" The woman asked. She had dyed white hair. Not blond, white. And tattoos that ran up and down her body like pistons. In the weak light, William could only make out that they seemed to be dragons and damsels.

"Let's have you throw up in the bushes. That way Billy and Bea won't have to clean it up tomorrow."

Monster's finger had left Maggie's breast. His hand was at his side, fingers no longer pointing.

The woman snapped her fingers to get William's attention and then used her hand to indicate the exact spot she wanted William to vomit. It happened to be under the window where Maggie and Monster were now arguing.

William nodded in appreciation, though he didn't have anything more to vomit. In the window above, Maggie and Monster were hugging closely now. The woman waited patiently. William dutifully tried to wretch out a few drops of bile. This seemed to satisfy the woman.

"I've been so drunk I can't talk, too," she said, as she rubbed his back. "That means you won't remember anything I say right now, will you?"

William shook his head.

Above him, he could hear Monster speaking in a hushed yell that finally broke through the wall.

"You're gonna stay down there. I fucking know it." Monster said. He spoke low but clear.

"This is my home, Monster. You're my home. My mom needs this van. Her truck broke down and they don't have enough money to fix it. This van can get them through the season. It all just happened. I need to do this."

"Your mom's a bitch."

"Don't call her that," Maggie said.

"You call her that all the time."

"I'm allowed to."

"Love is hard," the woman said to William. She was eavesdropping on Maggie and Monster, too. "But don't worry about Maggie and Monster. Those two are gonna make it. I just know it. Come on, grandpa, sit with me on the ground. Let's chat about life."

The woman sat Indian style on the concrete. She pulled William down next to her.

"You remind me of those old-time commercials with grandpas and cookies, where the grandpa is wise or something," the woman said.

Maggie must have said something to calm Monster down. William hadn't heard it because of the talking woman. Because when he stretched his neck to peek through the window, he saw that they'd made up. Monster had his hands down the front of her jeans and he bit the bottom of his lip as he did this.

The woman continued talking and found a rhythm to her monologue. It revolved around an ex-boyfriend, a college exam that she'd flunked and her failed dream of being an airline pilot. She jumped around these three topics without transition, without segues, except when she felt the need to condescendingly comment on the cuteness of William's advanced age.

William quit listening to the woman's words. He watched her mouth as it moved, up and down, her lips red and full. She was telling the story of her life but she seemed to be only interested in telling that story to herself. William drifted.

He was back at Sire Foods. It was early afternoon, maybe three o'clock. The excessive coolness of the air conditioning hit him and it felt good. A few small beads of sweat formed on his temple and he wiped off the dew with the sleeve of his yellow cardigan. He looked around for Pedro but didn't see him. According to his watch, Pedro should still be on the clock. He knew Pedro's schedule, he

.new when he went on lunch or break. William went through the turnstile and began to walk the aisles, scanning for his friend. Later, he would wonder why he hadn't noticed certain things when he had spent a lifetime learning how to notice, learning how to eavesdrop. His thirty years of working as a janitor in a high school had honed his skills at spotting the abnormal amid the mundane. He knew, from a twinge of an eye, to a placid smile, to a jerk of the neck, who was on what, who had taken what, who had fucked whom. Context was his domain.

Had he just been more aware, less frantic in his need for whiskey and peaches and Pedro, he would have noticed the four men who entered right after he did. He would have noticed that they were dressed alike, that they wore combat boots and seemed unduly sweaty, with small dots for pupils in the center of their eyes, and with steely expressions, all of one purpose, as if their faces had become masks.

He went to the produce section and looked at the bushels of peaches. He could smell the nectar but didn't linger to enjoy it. He didn't see Pedro there nor did he see that two of the men had left the front of the store and were making their way to the back office, where the safe was, while the other two stayed near the exits and the check-stands.

He went to the liquor aisle, which was adjacent to that office where the manager on duty could, ostensibly, look down from the double-sided mirror and spot would-be alcohol thieves, but Pedro wasn't there, either.

Then, relief. Over the top of a display of cheap vodka, William could see Pedro near the door that led upstairs to the office. Pedro must have taken his break early and spent it in the office looking over the store. William took a deep breath and relaxed.

He heard someone yelling near the check-stands and he looked to see what the commotion was.

He saw the men. He heard the nerves in their strained, metallic voices.

Then he saw the two other men, now racing down the aisle that led to the office door.

He saw them, finally, and he saw the guns.

Then the men disappeared from his sight, blocked by the angle and the large corner sales display of an assortment of beans: kidney, lentils and refried. He looked back to Pedro, who was still lingering by the door, fiddling with his cell phone. William realized that they were running towards his friend. Or rather, they were running towards the office door that led to the safe. He realized that Pedro was in their way.

Pedro noticed William through the vodka gloss, the liquid in the bottles distorting both men like a carnival fun house, and waved at him, giving him a look of *what happened?* This was because William usually shopped much earlier. But Sammy had died. William opened his mouth, but nothing would come out. He pointed to the aisle, to the men running towards Pedro.

He gesticulated wildly, but that just made Pedro keep his focus on William instead of what he ought to be focusing on.

Again, William opened his mouth and again, nothing but stifled air came out. He grabbed his throat and choked himself in disgust.

Pedro was motioning for William to calm down and relax. He made a gesture of *one minute*, bent down to pick up a piece of garbage from the floor, then William heard an exchange of unclear voices like jabs in the air, then a gun shot, and then a low, baying moan.

William stood staring through the vodka. The store went unearthly silent. Just that moan, echoing off the promotional displays and the bread racks and the hominy, off the harsh light and the cold tile. Only the moan was audible in the large, modern building where everything could be bought.

Something broke the silence. Something told William to move. He bent down and covered his ears and thought of war, of the great war that made his father a monolith of a man, elegiac and huge, of Vietnam that made him angry and self-immolate, of the war on terror that made him distrust and apathetic.

I know nothing of war, he told himself.

He found himself crawling along the cold tile, olive green and gold, a lost artifact from the mine of the seventies, he crawled away from the whiskey and down the paper-goods aisle. He listened for the men and for the moan. All sound seemed to have evaporated. He kept crawling. He saw the cheap bleach on the bottom rung, the generic napkins and paper plates on sale two-for-one. The products banished to the lowest shelf. Finally, he reached the end of the aisle.

He could see Pedro's feet, bent like freshly cut flowers. He crawled to him and then saw the pool of crimson and the subsequent rivulets that flowed slowly from Pedro's chest. He was still breathing. William touched his cheek and it was warm. Pedro's eyes opened and he stared directly into William's. There was no panic present. His breathing was slowing but he kept his gaze on William. He was saying something to William, even though no words came out. Then, Pedro closed his eyes and William felt the warmness leave his cheeks. Pedro was dead.

William closed his friend's mouth, which had dropped open. It was William's fault.

Time seemed to expand for William, who thought nothing of the armed men who had headed up the office stairs. Instead, William began recanting all the tragedies that he had endured, that helped fill the pages of his life.

But nothing came to him. His personal tragedies meant nothing. They seemed so cold and small and distant. There was nothing more to look back at, there were no more thoughts to have. The past seemed lost.

William held Pedro's head in his hands and found himself stroking the man's dark thatch of coarse hair.

"I...I...I...I...I...I." William tried, but he couldn't say anything more. Pedro's face was blank and ashen. William frantically searched the man's body. All he found was a cheap wooden rabbit's foot attached to a chain around his neck. He knew what it was. It was from Pedro's son who lived far away in Mexico. William snapped the amulet off the chain and put it in his pocket.

"William," Maggie said. "Are you okay?"

William was sitting on the ground, staring blankly. The noise of the party was growing. The woman who'd been speaking to him was gone. William was freezing cold.

"Are you okay?" Maggie asked again.

He nodded.

"Sorry about the delay. I had to tell some friends goodbye. You know how it is."

William felt the wooden rabbit's foot inside his pocket and then pushed himself off the ground and followed Maggie to the van.

6

"I haven't been back home since I arrived in the US. The end is the beginning, I suppose."

William could smell the cocaine on her. It was sterile, like a hospital. A fucked up hospital. Her jaw clenched and then released.

"Not that I should be boring you with any of this. I should just shut up. But, it's a big deal. That's all I'm going to say. I've resisted this for too long. It's time. So what about anything and everything. I mean it would be so easy to stay in that bar forever and it'd be fine, too. So fucking what? You just sort of have to deal with it and then move on. You can't change the past and frankly, I don't know if I'd even want to. You know?" She laughed. She knew she wasn't making sense. Then she tried her best to stop her verbal tirade and turned up the music.

After a mile, she simply talked over the music, mostly to herself. Nervous words about the future and the past. William grabbed his journal from his bag and flipped through it.

June 20th, 1991, Apartment 8, Pedro the Cashier, has had a son. He weeps with pride and happiness. He praises

Jesus and blesses everything. He talks to his wife over the phone for hours forcing her to describe his newborn's eyes and cheeks and cleft chin. It's his third child. His older boy Luis, then Marta and now little Teofilo. He would do anything to be there with her, but he can't go back. I must find out why and help him back there. I must do this. It is my duty.

This is why I'm helping Maggie, thought William. Promises made in the dark, under Pedro's window decades earlier. William meant what he wrote. He flipped to another entry.

May, 19th, 1995, Apartment 8, Pedro the Cashier, calls his wife back home and promises her that he will come home soon. But then he hangs up and tells his girlfriend that he can't go back, not even for his boy Luis. I can hear in his voice that he feels lost and trapped. He wants to know his son, but knows that to give his son what's best for him, he needs to stay here and work and make money. I wish I could help. I wish I could find a way to get him back there. Maybe this is my duty.

June 3rd, 2000, Apartment 8, Pedro my Best Friend. His son, my godson, refuses to speak to his own father! I get angry thinking about it, as if Luis doesn't know, isn't aware, of the sacrifices that his father has made for him. Living in a foreign country where he must work below his station, where he has to bag groceries for people like me. The boy hates him but I wonder if that is just a child's hate, if it's hate that doesn't understand what parents do for their children. I wish I could help him get there, even for a short time, I wish I could make it so that Luis understands his father. And then there's the thing I *feared most happening. Pedro is moving from his apartment. I don't know where his new apartment is. I will only see him at the Sire's now.*

"You journal?"

William looked over at Maggie and nodded. Though he felt journaling was too weak a description.

"I used to journal until I realized that I had nothing interesting to say. Only Americans journal. It's sort of narcissistic if you think about it. 'Look at me and my problems!' If I write them down they seem bigger than they are and then I get to feel important for a few lines of cursive."

William stared at her dumbfounded.

"I don't mean you. I mean me, or other people." Maggie looked straight ahead and quit talking. William placed his journal back in his bag.

William closed his eyes and tried to sleep. If he were home right now, if it had been a few days earlier, if the people and birds had kept on living, he would be doing the crossword puzzle on the kitchen table, struggling to remember if a wooded flatland was *lea* or *lee*. His eyes would darken with exhaustion as he struggled to discover the right word. Sammy would have the rose blanket draped over her silver cage. He would finish the crossword and then try and talk himself out of sitting under Maggie's window and listening to her voice or her silence. He thought of her. Her forays into acting, practicing a Chekov monologue or Stella's pathetic rant, her angry diatribes at men, those stunted phone calls home, her grandiose predictions to Lupe and Monster. She tried so magnificently at life.

William peeked his eye open. She was really there. Sitting next to him. Her eyes looked watery and heavy. He was certain she could feel his gaze.

"What are you looking at?" she laughed. "I'm trying to not bother you. But who are you? Other than some guy who needs to get to Mexico. But why? You show up on my door drunk at like midnight and hand me a note. Who does this? You do. I wonder why, is all. But you can't tell me because you can't talk. You tell me some friend of yours died and you have to get back to where he lived. But really, you just sit there. Quiet. Saying nothing." Maggie looked straight ahead and stopped talking. She looked at William out of the corner of her eyes. "I should let you know that I'm not a very good person."

William sat upright in his seat. A long time paused before Maggie spoke again. She breathed in and out like a swimmer just up for air.

"I haven't seen my daughter in fifteen years. I gave birth to her and then I left her there when I came north. She's where we're going. Or she's where I'm going. It's the real reason I agreed to do this. Drive you to Mexico."

William knew this. He'd heard about her daughter Jessica many times over the years. Without thinking, he reached over and patted her knee. She looked at his hand and he removed it after the third tap and placed it back into his own lap.

"I'm not a good person," she repeated.

They drove on and the lights of the eternal Los Angeles boon eventually gave way to the yellow haze of home-office lights emanating from the single-family homes of Orange County. The landscape remained the same but the context had changed. Christian goodness was omnipresent. Disneyland fireworks wreaked havoc on the sky. Billboards didn't advertise safe sex (instead, they advertised Bahamian vacations and chain restaurants) and were always in English. When they finally passed Laguna, William could see the ocean and he sat up in his seat. Behind him were the steep cliffs of San Clemente where the rich built houses on stilts and slopes, and in front of him, an endless mess of tides and waves. He felt like Huck Finn might have on his first ride down the Mississippi.

Next was the netherworld of Camp Pendleton. It was too dark. It was menacing and foreboding, though William didn't know why. He shut his eyes for this stretch and when he came back to civilization, away from the armaments and Marine chants, back to where war was something to read about or watch on TV, he opened his eyes again and found that everything in Oceanside looked the same as it had in Orange County. They plunged forward into the dark night.

Somehow, near 9:00 PM, the 5 freeway was bumper to bumper just north of San Diego.

"The audacity of this. The utter audacity," muttered Maggie. William understood that the coke was wearing off. She hadn't done enough for a bad come down but he knew it wasn't going to be a pleasant hour. "I fucking hate traffic. I just want to get to where I'm fucking going." The cars formed a mass of red blinking brake lights and William thought it looked like a mosaic modern art piece. He reached for his backpack and pulled out his journal. He scribbled into it for a few seconds. Then ripped out the page and handed it to Maggie.

Let's get to know each other better. Favorite movie?
She sighed. "Oh, William. Really?"
William nodded firmly.
"Fine. Um, I don't know. If I were being graded I would say something like *The Godfather* or maybe *Scarface*. But, really, it's *Beauty and the Beast*. Not that Mexican girls ever get to be Belle. You?"
William wrote: *Casablanca. But really it's Dumbo.*
Maggie smiled. Up ahead she could see the gyrating glare of ambulances.
"So we're both cartoon softies. William, why don't you talk? I mean, it's not my business, but this is our road movie and in road movies two people feel safe enough to share secrets they wouldn't otherwise. Like what I said before, about my daughter. I didn't want to tell you that. I have great friends who don't know that about me. But we're on the road. The rules change."
William thought about his answer. He thought of Pedro first. If only he could have warned him. He thought of his mother's funeral, his tormentor and his saint, and the unspoken eulogy. He thought of women. The one's he might have loved.

William opened his mouth to speak. "I...I...I...I...I." He made that same stunted sound twenty times.

Maggie winced as it continued. "Okay, William. I get it." Maggie stopped and pointed up ahead.

"Look at that," she said. The car in the wreck was totaled. It lay in a crumpled metal mess on the far shoulder. Smoke rose up from the hood. Two people, looking shocked and awed, huddled under thin blankets, talking to the cops. "Damn. If somebody didn't die in that wreck, they sure should have."

7

They passed through the rest of San Diego without any more duress. Nearing the border, Maggie repeated that they needed to find a motel to sleep in for the night. "We want to get some good sleep before the real trip begins." She'd forgotten to get dinner but William didn't mind. He agreed that it was time to rest. They found a place just off the freeway.

In the dark, Maggie stared at the ceiling. The room was sparse in comfort. It smelled of wet leather. The bed was too stiff. Cracks littered the walls with tributaries. Maggie was sure a murder had taken place here or maybe just meth use. She let her mind worry itself into a frenzy. This room reminded her of the ones she'd stayed in on her way into the States, when it may as well have been a castle to her. She wished she had her own room but the motel had only one vacancy. He's okay, Maggie convinced herself. She closed her eyes willfully. She wanted more blow. Instead, she would demand sleep of herself.

She looked over at William, who appeared to sleep soundly in the bed to the left of hers. The bedspread was tucked under the back of his neck. The desert tan color somehow made him look whiter than he was. He looked peaceful asleep.

But William's sleep was disturbed. Up in the sky, satellites beamed down their signals on him as he curled in fetal position on the motel's twin bed. Then they beamed their lights elsewhere. Boys and girls watched television shows dance on their computer screens. Outside, the streets were empty. Babies cried and no one seemed to care. The whole of America was busy capitulating, feeling sorry for itself, trying to get the words out. It was busy trying not to die. The whole of America attempted to fast-forward through the commercials even as they wished they could rewind back and hear it all just one more time. The satellites – big, floating, metallic behemoths – glided harmlessly in the lack of gravity. They moved in their orbit with a confounding grace. A corona of the sun's light bounced off these façades and it was brilliant.

No one on earth noticed.

And then, something began to happen. The satellites, guided by a set of unseen hands began to shift their gaze away from the purple mountains majesty and towards some other place altogether. The whole of America didn't matter. It didn't even exist. It tried to recall nothing because there was nothing to recall. It failed to exist. The satellites had found a new place to shine.

William awoke with a start, his heart beating wildly. That damned dream again. Every time this dream invaded his sleep he felt disconcerted and wondered what it meant.

For the first time in a long time, he didn't want to go back to sleep. The morning hadn't yet seen the sun. William looked over at Maggie and watched her body rise and fall. His eyes blinked like small, impotent explosions in the darkness.

8

Maggie was up and waiting when William finally woke up again. He rubbed his eyes and looked at her.

"Morning. I woke up early and got donuts."

William got out of bed and grabbed a jellyroll on the nightstand and bit into it.

"I want to get going early. I have no idea if it's as interesting going into Mexico as it was going out of it, but an earlier start seems to be better. Not really sure why that is, but whatever."

William nodded.

The morning was unyieldingly bright. It poured through every window in the van and William had to keep squinting his eyes to look out the window. But he shaded his eyes as best he could and continued looking outside. Vendors appeared in droves selling trinkets, food, churros. Police were everywhere. People were walking where it didn't seem people should be walking. The cars themselves varied from old jalopies to work trucks to gleaming sedans. The pace was frenetic yet methodical, a virus that was spreading at the slowest transmission rate imaginable. The pedestrians kept their heads down, eyes on their shoes, their pace quick. The cops seemed bored, but ready to attack. There was a line of cars waiting to cross at the border. Maggie guided the van behind the last car.

"In case you're wondering, I'm legal. I have my green card. I can come and go as I please." She seemed to be saying this more to herself than to William. "So if they try and ask me shit or whatever, don't worry, William. I'll just show them my green-card and they can't say shit." The van inched forward. "Shit. Why the hell is there a line to go *into* Mexico?"

The sun was blinding William. It shot through the windshield even as it was still high in the east. He put down his visor but that didn't work. He shifted his attention out of his window but the glare found him there, as well. His legs began to shake.

"William, stop."

William stopped shaking.

Maggie could see the guard up ahead. "Typical macho Mexican cop. I wonder how much he's going to ask once he sees I'm with a white man."

They were the next vehicle in line to cross. William was now shielding the sun with his hands. He was trying to peer into Mexico, to see how much a few feet changed the landscape, but he couldn't see a thing. As they approached, the guard looked hard at Maggie and then at William. Maggie smiled at him. He waved them through. Then the sun shifted a bit and William could finally see what was in front of him.

Maggie eased the car into gear and they crossed the border. William looked hard for a change but he couldn't find one. Not just yet.

9

When Maggie was a child, Tijuana had been billed as the gateway city to the Oz of California. The last dangerous stop on the midnight train to some destined prosperity, television sets in every room, blue skies forever. It was a city of vice and promise. She remembered it with equal parts fear and admiration.

"I've never been here before," she said. William cocked his head. "I came in through Juárez, just across from El Paso." The traffic whirred around the van, cars like darting missiles. The kids selling ponchos and Chicklets banged on the windows of stopped cars. The billboards with white lawyers promising workers' comp jackpots did their best to hide the mountains that cut a swath through the city. Two teenagers fell out of a corner bar, congratulating themselves.

"It's nothing like I pictured it and it's exactly like I pictured it."

Such is life, thought William. He had never imagined this sprawling city with its mishmash of colors and smells, both robust and rotting. He had never imagined anything outside his tiny little dominion, outside of Sammy's cage and the cracked sidewalks on Fountain where the cockroaches lurked. He had never imagined a scene such as the one that lay before him. It was dirty, the grime palpable, similar to Los Angeles, but it moved in a way Los Angeles never could. The shacks that lined the hillsides, the children that lined the streets, the way traffic swerved in dissonant patterns, were a testament to survival, to something William innately understood but had never been able to articulate, even to himself. He found breathing difficult.

He remembered his mother telling him when he was young that his home would never be but down the street, that he hadn't the mettle to make it on his own. His brother would move away, raise a family, seek corporate gold. William would stay attached to the apron strings. She told him that and served him macaroni and cheese, then patted him lovingly on his head. What a lying bitch, William thought.

"What's wrong?" Maggie asked.

He shook his head and closed his eyes. Then he opened them and wrote something down.

"You want to eat. Here? No, William. It isn't safe. Not for you. We have to get away from the border. Trust me on this."

William shook his head. Safety meant nothing to him.

"William, we really shouldn't."

He shook his head more violently and pounded his fist on his seat.

"Okay. But if some drug dealer takes you hostage and steals your kidney, don't blame me." She looked for an exit from the highway. "We need to get supplies anyway. Maps, food. I need a cell that works here. We really did a horrible job of planning this."

They parked and walked towards a narrow pedestrian street lined with shops where tourists could buy duty-free Mexican arts and crafts. The street was mostly empty, despite the pleasant weather and eager shopkeepers, whose eyes widened when they saw William pass.

"Dead zone now," Maggie explained. "Drugs. Cartels. The donkey shows and drunken frat vibe are still here, but not like before. Whites are too afraid to come down. I don't blame them. Hell, I don't like being here." A dog ran past Maggie with a piece of stolen meat in his mouth. "What do you feel like eating?"

They found a small taco stand next to a store selling piñatas and sat down at a little circular table, watching the few tourists who happened by. William bit into his taco as he watched a woman in an oversized sun hat haggle for the lowest possible price from a serape vendor.

She's done this before, William thought with just a slight pang of envy.

Maggie watched William closely. He was a child at a circus, in complete awe of everything. She took a sip of beer and the last bite of her taco. She found herself wanting to be away from him.

"Listen, I'm going to go and get a few things at the store down the street. Wait here for me, okay?"

William nodded.

Five minutes later he was meandering through a piñata shop, marveling at the different shapes and sizes of the papier-mâché items.

"This one's very popular," the shopkeeper said to William without solicitation. He spoke as if his English was quite poor, save for this one, well-rehearsed phrase, which had almost no accent to it. "Very popular, indeed." He pointed at what appeared to be a burro with multicolored frills flowing off the body. William smiled. The shopkeeper smiled. Not knowing what to do, William backed up.

"I'll give you two burros and one horse for the price of an elephant," the shopkeeper said, raising his voice. "We sell candy, too. Very cheap. Please, stay."

William took a few steps back.

"Okay, okay. You take the two burros and I throw in three bags of candy. Deal?"

William turned to leave and he tripped over a giraffe. He tried to balance himself on a shelf of smaller piñatas but he only managed to take the whole shelf and its contents down with him to the concrete floor.

"Why you do this? Why you do this?" The shopkeeper placed his hands on cheeks in dismay. William got up quickly and tried to arrange the fallen piñatas in some sort of order.

"Look, look just buy the two burros and it's okay."

He put his head down, turned on his heels and exited the store.

"You break, you buy," the shopkeeper yelled. William didn't turn around, but he could hear the man bark desperate bargains and minor threats in broken English as William walked briskly down the street.

He kept walking farther down the street, away from the taco stand, too afraid to turn around and see if the shopkeeper was chasing after him. Finally, he felt it was safe to stop. He was out of breath, and as he looked around, he realized he was a bit lost, having taken a few twists and turns. He took a few deep breaths. Nothing had changed other than geography. He was still running from people on the streets. There had been a small part of him that thought he might change when he crossed the border that the mere act of leaving all he knew would reconfigure the molecules and usher in a brave new world of behavior.

No, he thought. He was just a man afraid of piñatas. Defeated, William sat down on the ground and put his hand underneath his chin.

"Excuse, me, but you will have to leave this corner immediately," said a voice in the smoothest Spanish.

William turned and looked up and saw a man made out of silver. He seemed to have appeared from thin air.

"I never speak. With you I have broken my vow of absolute silence. I hope you understand what this means."

He waited for William to respond.

"I will tell you then. It means I see in you a threat to my dominance of this corner."

William had no idea what to do. He resisted the urge to re-tie his shoelaces. He couldn't think of anything else to do.

The man was dressed in a tuxedo, also painted silver. William remembered seeing someone like him on Hollywood Boulevard, near Batman and Marilyn Monroe. He smiled. No matter how far he left Los Angeles, it didn't seem to want to leave him.

"I can't compete with you. There. I have said it."

William cocked his head.

"Even with the silver, I can't compete with you. Those eyes are too sad. The white skin too damn interesting. Rather ingenious. I wish I had thought of it – a white mime working the corner in Tijuana. I can't compete. But I would only ask that you move away from this corner. There are endless corners in this wicked city. I have worked this corner since the first breath of the Aztec tongue twisted together to form the sun and the moon."

William winced at this.

"Anyway," the man continued, "this corner means everything to me. It provides me my home, my artistry, my reason for being. I come here from the east. Sometimes I tell people, when I choose to break my vow of silence, that I ride the sun west each dawn to reach this corner but that's not true. I have an old Chevy that a white man – maybe you know him?"

William shook his head. The silver man dug for a coin in his pocket.

"Anyway, this white man, very *stupído*, paid me money to 'steal' his car. Insurance money, I guess. So I took it and built a new engine two summers ago. Now she purrs like *un gato*. I take the main highway, lots of traffic, cars for miles and miles and then get off at the exit with the four juniper trees, exit 14 I think. I make three left turns, two right turns, pass a used car dealership, three McDonald's, twelve bars of various repute, two police stations filled with liars and thieves, and also criminals, a pack of stray mongrels, a hopeless mother with dead children at her feet, and all the silly politics of these silly times before I reach this corner and undertake my vow of stillness. Which I have just broken."

William sat silent looking up at him.

"And still I don't get an answer?"

The silver man began flipping the coin over and over. He never once looked at it as it rose and fell in the air and he never once dropped it.

"I have told you more about myself in the last five minutes than I have said in the last twenty years of my life. And all you give me is that stupid smile?"

William pushed himself from off the ground. He put his hand on the silver mime's shoulder and with his other hand, offered him back his corner.

"You are a fierce warrior," the silver man said. Then he stood atop the box he traveled with and froze.

William reached into his wallet and put a dollar bill in the jar the silver mime used to collect tips. Then he turned and walked back down the street and he couldn't help but smile.

10

As she walked towards the taco stand, Maggie feebly attempted to refold the map she'd just bought. When she couldn't get the map just right, she shoved it back into the bag with the other groceries she had purchased. She pulled out her new prepaid cell phone and fiddled with it.

When she got to the taco stand, William wasn't there. She ordered another taco and beer and took her seat at the same table they'd eaten at earlier. A woman with two children, one in a stroller with a flat tire, the other one firmly in her hand, stopped and stared at Maggie. Maggie ceased chewing and stared right back. The woman sighed heavily, then squeezed the hand of her toddler, both to make sure he was still there and to prove ownership, and then continued down the street.

The faint odor of car exhaust and general din of noise and disorder were subtle, but never out of reach. It had been fifteen years since she'd been in her homeland. Part of her was sure that some bomb – spiritual, actual, mental – would explode the minute she crossed over. The truth was, no one cared that she was here. She was invisible, indistinguishable. She was just another Mexican girl with American tendencies sitting on a bench in TJ drinking a beer. There was nothing to be afraid of and nothing to be excited about. It was like sex, that big mysterious behemoth she had whispered about for years and years, hinted at, flirted towards, was weary of. Then she had it. He, whoever he was, slipped it inside of her and for one spectacular moment it lived up to the hype. It was painful and fraught and made her yearn for the boy, so much so that she dug her nails into his back and took off skin. Then it was over, faster than the Mexican mouse and he playfully slapped her for hurting his back.

She took the last bite of the cold taco, looking out at the pastel mess.

Then William returned. He waved at Maggie from the street.

She waved back.

"Where were you?"

Down the street, he motioned.

"See anything interesting?"

He shrugged.

"Here, finish my beer. I have to drive."

11

The van plunged east down the 2. The desert of the southwest was laborious and unforgiving, a dead morass of nothingness. William took in the utter extremes of yellows and browns. It was an effigy of a landscape. The beer was good for William. It calmed him.

He pointed to a steep butte and let his eyes grow wide with exaggerated awe.

"I'm sorry?" After a moment, she realized what he was hinting at. "I don't agree. It's drab and it's boring and it's colorless."

He shook his head.

"I think so. It's nothing but carcasses. And no amount of arm flailing is going to change my mind."

Maggie looked outside her window. For a second, she was fifteen again, on the move. Their man, the one who was to take them across, a spurious Mexican with a legal citizenship card, was shifty from the first time she had met him. But he charged her and Lupe only half what the others charged – three thousand dollars. And that was all she and Lupe could afford. They met at the safe house with the big red door – Maggie remembered that big red door, it stood out in the desert – and the man kept telling them it wasn't the right night. Three more nights of it not being the right night passed. Then, it was. They left on foot after 10:00 PM. It was dark and moonless. The backpacks felt like they weighed more than either girl, the water bottles hung off their belts like Smith & Wessons. The three of them, two girls and their jittery guide, made their way into the desert night and the man promised them great tales of Texas triumphs. Then, three hours into the desert, just across the border, the lights of a helicopter emanated from miles away. The man panicked. He told them to wait there, that he had to go and see something. He promised the girls he would be back in a few minutes.

He never came back. He ditched them in a meth-fueled panic attack somewhere near the border, somewhere just like this unlivable expanse. No lights. Just miles of desert in every direction. The night never ending. Maggie holding Lupe so close, animal calls encircling them, the freezing night air, the sounds of distant gunshots, the American border police and rattlesnakes ready to bite, certain death of some variety was imminent.

An eighteen-wheeler stormed past from the opposite direction. Maggie looked over at William, then back outside.

With a sudden jerk, William pointed to a patch of faded beige sand littered with a dramatic rock formation, the type of formation, with the right erosion and shadow, where a religious figure might be found in the crevices.

"Sorry, William. It's boring and flat and unlivable. And it's dangerous."

They drove on through the desert for over an hour. William dutifully watched the gas needle. Buzzards circled something in the distance. The cars next to them never seemed to begin or end.

12

Maggie called Monster on the prepaid cell phone she picked up in Tijuana. William felt comforted as he listened to her talk. He had, on numerous occasions, been in a similar scenario while sitting under Maggie's window.

"No, she did not." Maggie said, almost in a shout.

William knew this meant Monster's ex-girlfriend had called or written or done some other grievous thing to disrespect Maggie. He looked outside and saw a car with three men inside. One looked alarmingly similar to Pedro. He felt his neck for the wooden rabbit's foot, just to be sure. He realized he needed to come up with something to show the young man, Pedro's now fatherless son, some story to illustrate just how much his father loved him, when they finally met.

William reached into the back seat and picked up his journal. He skimmed the pages and read from entries as if they were gospel. He flipped through numerous pages, wanting to find just the right one.

June 20, 2005

Pedro has come from nowhere to seize firmly something his own, something altogether American. He has found his niche and as I watch from the aisle, I couldn't be more proud. He has truly found some sort of oasis in the desert. He has developed woman, culture, piety and humor all on his own terms. I watch him and I know goodness.

A little heavy handed, thought William.

"I'm leaving Monster." Maggie said. She lit a cigarette that William didn't know she possessed.

William put down his journal. He looked over at her with a raised eyebrow,

"I'm done with him."

She loved men like a tourist, William understood. She saw the best in them, was fascinated by their history and etymology, took tours and learned the topography, the geography. Then she left after three days, or a week, or maybe three months. She took pictures, she bought postcards, but she always left.

"He has a problem with drugs. I deserve something more than that."

William slept hard with his head pressed against the window. Maggie chain smoked next to him, wondering when and if she should call her mother and tell her that she was headed home. She opted for some later date. She thought of her mother, of the woman and the dream, and then she didn't want to think of her, or of any mother, ever again and through sheer force of will she thought of nothing. The van seemed to drive itself.

13

This time, William, sleeping as the van crunched its tires over sand blown in from a westerly wind, was standing in the middle of a busy highway. His hands were raised up, one in either direction, commanding the speeding vehicles to stop. Amazingly, each vehicle stopped just before hitting the one in front of it. Thousands of travelers stopped by the sheer force of William's outstretched hands. The highway seemed to have infinite lanes and it went in both directions forever. Most of the vehicles were semis, barreling goods from one side of the country (but what country?) to the other. The men, and a few women, got out of the elevated cabs to look at him, this crazy man with his arms still raised up, rigid, even as his body remained flaccid in repose. Who was he to make them all stop? Somehow, William could see inside the trucks, the large semis, his vision penetrating the heavy steel of each body. Mounds of cocaine, scores of families, arm chairs, soccer balls, widgets and tractors.

The truckers stood idle by their rigs and waited for William to give them an explanation or maybe direction. William felt his mouth dry up. He was about to say something but instead, in the long, weary faces of the drivers, William could see to the date when and how each was going to die. He realized this suddenly, when a man near the front, wearing a Yankees cap and driving refrigerated beef, stood up and asked him what the hell he was doing. William couldn't answer him. He was too distracted by the knowledge that the burly man would be dead in three months, asleep at the wheel traveling the 10 through the slick mountain passes just east of Albuquerque, as the man's wife was calling on his cell to tell him some small piece of family good news.

Next, a woman came to ask him when it would be safe to travel again, as she was late with her cargo of a family of Oaxaca apple pickers headed north for Washington. She was lean, with a stretched white face and designer clothing. William shook his head and tried to extinguish the image of her death at the age of seventy-three, her hip too fragile for the hard ceramic of the shower floor. Neither of her daughters would attend her funeral, a silent protest against a long-ago wrong.

Two blond twins, maybe sixteen, came to him next. They were identical and wore matching outfits of blue jeans and white T-shirts. They told him they were in a hurry. They had to get back home for school. William saw one poisoning the other, slowly, with arsenic, sick of being a half instead of a whole.

William felt disgusted. He wanted to warn every one of these people what lay ahead but he couldn't say a word. Each time he tried to speak, a new death entered his mind and disabled him. He saw cancer multiply and overtake organs and skin, he saw murders, some of passion, some of sport, and he saw the blank stares and empty eyes of those on some bridge, looking down into the swirling water, looking into the depths for some small sliver of solace.

The images hit him like flashbulbs, over and over, blinding him, taking away another of his senses. He made them stop and then exhaled. As he did, his sight was restored and he saw the entire highway in ruin. It was the largest paved road he had ever imagined, which seemed to stretch from the Atlantic to the Pacific, burned down by the most epic of fires. He saw the end of the large, infinite highway, going forever in either direction, and he couldn't warn them to get the hell off it, find a new route. He couldn't say a word.

"William, William," Maggie said, nudging him awake.

He popped up, alert.

"That was some dream."

He tried to hide his fear.

"What was it about?"

He shrugged and forced himself to yawn. Then he patted his stomach.

"Yeah, I could eat, too."

14

She found a dinky restaurant off some dirt road in the middle of nowhere. A small pack of dogs lifted their heads as the graveled footsteps of Maggie and William disturbed their sleep. Then the dogs dropped their heads back down and returned to basking in the sun.

"Looks as good as any," Maggie said.

An old woman sat them. She labored through each of her movements. The table was wobbly and uneven, the room itself seemed to be sliding slightly into an unseen hole. A battery of fruit flies hovered overhead. She explained that pork was on the menu today.

"Steak?" asked Maggie. The old woman shook her head. Maggie ordered the carnitas enchiladas. William nodded the same. The woman smiled. She had no teeth and her cheeks were hollow and wrinkled.

"Waitress gives me the creeps."

William shot her a look.

"What? I have a thing against old people. A sign of things to come and all that."

He looked at her with incredulity.

"Not you, William. You're not old like that. Listen, it's my thing, not yours. Not hers." Maggie pointed to the waitress who was pouring tea into a mug. "I have the problem."

William excused himself to use the restroom. He paced around the tiny bathroom with the dirt floor. The toilet was a covered hole in the ground dug eight feet deep. It smelled the way it ought to and William held his breath and finally, he had to exit.

William reentered the small diner. It was completely empty, except for Maggie and the waitress. Had it been when they entered? The screen door was coming off its hinge and the fruit flies had migrated near the cook's station. When he went to sit down, he was surprised to find the enchiladas were already served and that the little old waitress was sitting down in his seat, whispering something to Maggie. Her Spanish was breathy, as if her lungs didn't work and it came it out in quick, muted bursts followed by a few deep breaths that she needed in order to attempt to speak again.

"Don't be angry at the revolution. Don't be angry at the fight your father fought and died for. It was just. The fact that it has failed isn't his fault." Deep breaths.

Her long bony hands pointed at Maggie's face, shaking with Parkinson's.

"What he did was a just thing, but it was led by men who were only boys days before. Boys led it. Be angry with that, be eternally angry with any man who not only leads, but also leads us right into war. Be suspect at any men who choose to swashbuckle, for they are the ones least fit to lead."

The woman's hand stopped shaking.

"You will die under a starry sky, under a sky filled with bright shiny stars, with fifty stars if not endless stars, the same way I did and then you will see the fruits of your father's death and then you will know the freedom that has eluded you all this life." She put her hand on her heart and took in as much air as possible. She was winded.

The steam from the enchiladas wafted upwards. The waitress looked back over her shoulder and saw William standing there. She gave him a nod of recognition, then slowly pushed herself away from the table and went back into the kitchen.

Maggie waited to make sure the woman was out of earshot.

"That was so fucking creepy," she whispered.

William took a bite of the pork and spit it out. It was dry and possibly rancid.

"She just came up to me and started talking about the revolution. I have no idea which one. I think she thought I was her daughter or her sister or a voice in her head. I don't know. Let's just get the hell out of here."

The old woman peered from behind the corner. Her large coffee-stained eyes, dulled silver with cataracts, were staring right at William. He looked away from her. He took another bite of his food. He looked up again and she was still fixated on him. He tried smiling at her. She shook her head. She walked back over to his table.

"The food. Good?" she asked in broken English.

William nodded.

"Lies," she said. She studied William. "Maybe I was talking to the wrong person. We start small, then we grow big, then we end up small again. We tell stories, we start myths, we build gods, then we lose gods, then we talk to ourselves like crazy people. We end up small." Then she laughed and held out her hand.

William reached for his wallet and gave her cash.

Dust from the van pulling out of the dirt parking lot caused a plume of smoke. William watched it in the side mirror.

"See, that kind of shit is everywhere down here. That waitress is an older, slightly crazier version of my mother. Everyone has visions and dreams and little fortune-cookie pearls of wisdom to freak the goddamn living shit out of you. They have nothing to do, so they all go insane."

A pang of compassion hit William.

"They rant and rave and bullshit."

William nodded. Then he remembered his nightmare. His own vision of the soon-to-be dead. He wanted to forget all about the waitress and his dream.

"Totally disconcerting. Topanga hippies gone sour."

William had no idea what that meant but he continued to nod regardless.

He wrote something out on the scrap paper.

"Why did I leave my boyfriend?" She was quiet for a moment. "He was a bad man. He was a monster. I told you before he had a drug problem. What more do I have to say?" She lit a cigarette. "Anyway, none of that matters down here."

15

They had pulled over at a gas station somewhere in the high desert when Maggie's mother called. A cold wind blustered from the south and William felt his first chill in days. The numbers on the gas dispenser slowly flipped higher, the sound reminding him of being a kid with Duke Snider in the spokes of his bicycle. Maggie sat on the edge of the hood. The sun was right over her, casting her shadow over the windshield.

William had always heard her voice from his spot in the dirt below her window but he could never see her. Now he could see, but not hear. The stress in her face was obvious. A vein popped along her temple, her lips were pinched, even as she exchanged what appeared to be minor pleasantries with her mother. And then she nodded and was silent for a long time. Her face changed from tense to drained to almost horrified. She became abstract. She appeared at William's window and he rolled it down.

"I need paper and pen." William opened the glove compartment and gave her both items. "Okay,

Mama, okay. We'll get there as soon as we can. Probably sometime tomorrow afternoon. I know, I know. I'll hurry. I know, Mama. I have got to go. Bye."

Maggie sat in the driver's seat for a good two minutes, doing nothing.

"We have to go to Juarez to pick up my mother. One of my nieces ran away and crossed. Mama tried to stop her but she failed."

William took the pen and jotted down: *Is your niece okay?*

"Yes, we have family in El Paso."

Maggie rubbed her eyes until they were red.

"How the hell did she get this phone number?" Maggie asked. William thought the waitress may have had a hand in it but he kept that theory to himself.

"She said she wants to stop the *dispirited exodus*. She lost another one to the red, white and blue. She'll be fine. And she'll be in the back seat." After a moment, Maggie looked temporarily stricken. "Oh, god," she added. "She'll be in the back seat."

16

The mood changed after they returned to the road. Maggie seemed nervous. Her finger tapped the steering wheel in malevolent rhythms. William simply stared out the window for long stretches, watching for birds to dive.

"Juarez is hopeless. I can't believe I have to go back there."

William looked at her. This didn't sound like Maggie at all. It sounded soft, childlike, revelatory.

He wanted to help but couldn't do anything. He reached into his bag and pulled out his journal.

"That woman said I would die under a crescent moon. And that I would see the freedoms that my father's death gave me. First, my father isn't dead. Second, people die all the time in Juarez and how the fuck am I supposed to know when the hell the moon is crescent?"

William flipped through the journal, reading bits of people's lives, trying to find something in his old words, but wasn't sure what. But it only made him miss Pedro, so he shut the book and placed it under his seat.

"You know what? I'm single again. I say we go out tonight. Have a night on the town. You and me. Dance, drink. Maybe meet some interesting people of the opposite sex. Then tomorrow, we get up early and start the trip to Juarez, pick my mother up, try not to kill her, find your friend's son, then head to my tiny hometown where I'll have no choice but to confront all that I want to forget. Then it's back to LA, where we can happily resume our small, insignificant little lives." Maggie extended her hand for William to shake. "Sound like a plan?"

He shook it firmly. He enjoyed her speeches.

"Perfect. Now, let's get the hell out of wherever the hell we are."

After the sun went down they got off the highway and found a fifty-peso motel. The woman behind the counter told them where they could find some food.

"What about a place to go dancing?" Maggie asked. The woman said she didn't know any such place but there were a few bars she could recommend.

They dropped off their bags in their rooms, cheap enough to each get their own, then went into the small town and ate. It was a lonely town. A few locals sat outside of empty shops chewing tobacco. A pack of kids played war down the dirt street. The air had turned from brisk to cold. Maggie shivered as they walked away from the restaurant, back towards the van. She looked like the town, William thought, desolate and windblown.

He remembered when he last saw her look like that. She was in front of her apartment in the rain, a rare May rain, after a fight with Monster. They had just started dating. William watched from his window as blood ran down her chin. Banshee hair and swollen eyes. Her chest was exposed as it pressed through the thin wet cotton of her white T-shirt. She yelled obscenities at Monster long after his El Camino had driven away. She danced on the small patch of lawn with clenched fists.

This time, instead of closing the curtains, William handed her his jacket.

"Give me an hour," she told William, when they returned to their rooms after dinner. William watched the 6 placard wiggle a bit after she shut the door. He went across the hall to his 7 and for the first time since Long Beach, had a moment to himself.

As he stared at the chipped mint green paint of the ceiling above his twin bed, Sammy came to his mind, as did Pedro. Then his mother, his father. Maybe he could see the dead, he thought.

"C-C-C-C." He wanted to say *Christ*. The expression, not the man. He wanted to say it as one mutters something private and inane, but nothing came out and he felt foolish even trying. He turned on the television and a woman was crying and screaming at the top of her lungs for everything and everyone to just stop.

Maggie dabbed a little makeup under her eyes, trying to obscure her exhaustion. Her birthday was in two months and she had a secret fear that she was too small to actually exist and that the older she got the smaller she shrunk, so that she would be a mere speck by the time she was fifty. She rotated blame for this – her mother, Mexico, her gender, America, destiny, God, godlessness and now age.

She brushed the long strands of her hair in the lopsided mirror just over the dresser. She told herself she just needed a man for the night. A minute later she was knocking on William's door.

The motel worker had given them directions to a few local bars in the vicinity.

Two brothers operated the first bar. It had small groups of people cowering in the corners, as the brothers drank more and more tequila. Maggie and William stopped in the doorway, just as the older brother, whose mustache was bushy and twisted with wax, swung for his younger brother, barely missing his shaved head.

"They drink more than they sell," said one of the cowering onlookers. They left just as the younger brother landed an open faced slap against his brother's back.

Down the street, the second bar wasn't much better. No one was there and the female bartender was sobbing in the corner of the bar.

"Get the fuck out of here," she said. "Just get the fuck out of here and never come back." Maggie looked over her shoulder at the slumped figure and saw the sheath of hair that covered the woman's face. She winced with compassion, then ushered William out of the door.

The third bar seemed to be the best option. It was run by a Mexican man with skinny legs and a large belly. His name was Sal, as indicated by the nametag that was pinned to his collared shirt. His bartender was a local kid, Miguel, with slicked-back hair and an overabundance of energy. He was a blur of washing glasses, dusting countertops, filling empty spaces anywhere he could find him.

"That was exhausting," Maggie said. They both agreed this seemed as good a place as any.

They sat at the end of the bar and watched a soccer game. A couple of local drunks were watching, too. Pleasant enough. Sal, behind the bar, leaned against the railing across from William.

"What the hell brings you this deep into Mexico?"

Maggie was a bit taken aback by his lack of an accent. He sounded American.

"He's my uncle. My escort home."

"Your uncle, huh?"

"By marriage."

"I don't see a ring."

"Divorced. But we're still close," she said.

"Your uncle keeps quiet."

"Most of the time." She waited for Sal's rebuttal. When he stayed quiet, she added: "Now that we've passed your test, how about a drink?"

"Sure, darling."

"Two Jamesons. Beer back."

Sal's lips twisted into a wicked smile. William felt uncomfortable. It wasn't even clever flirting, he thought.

The first three drinks went down easy. As he circled the pool table, William let his hands caress the mahogany edges. Maggie had moved on from awkward banter and was now grabbing Sal's arms after each joke he told. Her head reared up like a ram about to batter and then fell dramatically back down to her chest. Three men conspired over a bottle of tequila in the corner under the television set that played the soccer game. William rolled the eight ball against the side of the table and watched as it caromed. He felt his sense of awareness coming back to full strength, like it was before Pedro was killed, like it had been all of his life.

He knew the men were whispering about him. About his whiteness. He knew in this light, this flickering neon of noir and booze, he was shady and different. He liked it. He kept rolling the eight ball, over and over, watching the patterns it formed by accident.

The fourth drink hit him hard. He let the eight ball drop with a heavy thud into the corner pocket. He stared at nothing in particular. He missed his apartment. His routine. He felt too aware. A fervid sense of panic hit him but he was too drunk to do anything about it.

He walked back over to Maggie.

"William!" She threw her arms up, cheering. "Are you okay?"

William shook his head.

"You're staggering."

"Take a seat, William," Sal said. He was sitting in the chair William had vacated.

Maggie gave Sal a look only bartenders know. The casual roll of the eyes when a patron has had two too many. Again.

"Listen," Sal said, getting up from the seat and gently guiding William into it. "Why don't we get out of here? Go back to my place. I can put William on the couch and, you know. We can just move the party elsewhere."

"You can just leave?"

"I've got Miguel behind the bar."

Miguel smiled at her as he washed a glass. Maggie looked around. The group of three men had grown to a group of six and they were arguing about the teams on the television. She had been in rooms like this forever.

"Let's go."

Sal's house was in a densely populated village. He lived in a small two-bedroom house that had a nice view of a desert valley.

"I can get to Arizona in thirty minutes. I go all the time. Most of my friends live there but for me this is home."

"Is it tough to get back and forth?"

"Not at all. I'm American. Born in Fresno."

They sat on his small porch overlooking the valley and drank red wine.

"I am, too. Married a gay guy for a green card. He got a wife and I got citizenship. Best three years of my life."

William was listening as he sobered up on a couch inside the house, just under the porch window. He could see the back of their heads through that window. Above them, the moon was huge and red.

He knew what would happen. They would continue to talk and then they would move in close to one another. And then they would have sex. Or maybe they'd first go inside the house to Sal's bedroom before fucking. He imagined what each was feeling right at that moment, when small revelations were being whispered, when one had to expose one's character carefully, when one had to walk that fine line between ego and humility that one always has to walk when trying to seduce another. He wanted to feel it just once.

He shut his eyes but sleep wasn't coming.

He lifted his body off the couch and went to the kitchen. He drank water from the fridge and reached for the back door, which led to a small alley.

"Where you going, William?" Sal asked, still on his front porch. William turned to him and shrugged. Sal went through his house and met William in the alley.

The two men stared at each other.

Maggie came outside, too. She slid her hands around Sal's waist and rested her head on his back. The red wine had flushed her face, which now matched the color of the moon. William turned back around and headed for the street off the alley.

"Why don't you stay here? We can all go back inside. Play some cards or something."

William saw Maggie clasp her hands firmly at his belt buckle. He then turned around and started walking down the alley.

"Fuck," Sal said quietly. "He can't walk around by himself. Stay here. I'll go get him."

Sal jogged down the alley until he met William, just as he turned the corner toward the main street.

"Let's just go back to my place," Sal said. He slapped William playfully on the shoulder. "Are you upset with me? Or Maggie?"

William shook his head.

"Then what is it?"

He continued to shake his head *no*.

"Listen. Where do you want to go? At least tell me that. Maybe I can steer you in the right direction."

William stopped. He faced Sal. Then he wrapped his arms around himself, like Maggie had just done to Sal.

"Okay. I get it. I'll see what I can do."

17

Sal drove them down the hill into the flats of the village. His car was a truck with oversized wheels and a hemi-engine roar. William felt like he was riding in a tank. Through the window, the humble homes and buildings were a series of dark bumps against that moonlit sky and William imagined himself on a military probe, seeking out the enemy in a rebel camp.

"What are we doing?" Maggie whispered somewhat carelessly, cognizant that William, still drunk enough, was amusing himself with something or other and wouldn't hear what she was saying.

"He wants companionship."

"How do you know? He doesn't speak."

"Because I know."

"So, we're going to a singles bar? For bingo night or canasta?" She looked over her shoulder. William had his finger shaped like a pistol and was shooting at would-be assassins outside.

"God. A hooker. Of course."

Sal's face conveyed to Maggie that her assertion was correct. She rolled her eyes.

"No. Come on. He can go look at porn like everyone else."

"Not in my house. Listen. We'll drop him off. Give him an hour. You and I can stay in the car or go for a walk. Then he comes back, we go back to my place. No harm done. He's happy. We're happy. Look at that big red moon. It's begging us to let him do this."

"A begging moon. At least it's not a crescent moon," Maggie said. "Fine." She turned back to William.

"Sal's taking you to a *classy* whorehouse. Naturally, I am opposed, but if this is the sort of thing you want to do, by all means. Who am I to judge?"

William looked at her blankly. Then his eyes moved over to Sal. A very subtle smile found spread across William's face. Sal reached into his pocket.

"Here's forty. That should do the trick. Be back in one hour. I'll wait for you here in the car. The place is just up that stone path, past the pink house. Third door on the right. You can't miss it. It's a big red door."

William opened the door to the car. He was nervous. He tipped his head to both of them before ascending the path that Sal had directed him toward.

***

Sal's hand moved from the gear clutch to Maggie's thigh. She let it. The image of the big red door was trapped in her mind, even as Sal deftly unbuckled her jeans and slid them around her ankles, lifting her ass up with his right hand. The vinyl of the seats felt damp and cold.

Even as Sal's fingers made their way inside of her, Maggie was thinking of the big red door and the meth addict who ushered her into the United States. That morning, fifteen years ago, Maggie ate eggs the woman served her in the house behind that door. Each bite was reluctant and deliberate. She knew when the eggs were finished, and the goat's milk, she would have to round up Lupe and head out the door and into the desert with her guide.

**

William knocked first and no one answered. It was a yellow porch with ferns hanging from jute suspenders and a menagerie of succulents on either side of the door. William remembered his father's love of botany, the makeshift lab he had built in the backyard shed where he attempted to find the perfect hybrid of a fern that needed no sun. William would stand in the doorway and his father would ask him to step out of the light so that he could see what he was doing. William the boy sunk back in the shadows.

He would like these jutes, William thought. He twisted the rope a bit and it spun back and forth until it finally found its center.

The welcome mat was in English and had ten cats in various positions whose tails spelled out: ENTER WITH HAPPINESS. William didn't want to step on it.

He knocked again and this time the door opened. Three young women wrapped their arms around different parts of his body like serpents on a vine. They were young. The leader of the house came and shooed the girls away.

"Little pests." She smoked a cigar. She was drinking brown liquor from a plastic cup. Scotch maybe. "How the fuck does a gringo like you find a place like this? Jorge? Bandino? Sal?"

William looked up at Sal's name.

"Sal. Well, isn't that lucky for you. Let's begin the lineup. Girls."

And the girls flocked around their madam like imprinted ducklings.

***

Now Sal has his hands on Maggie's breasts. His breath was heavy and Maggie breathed it in. It smelled of peppermint, but rustic and hearty. His hands gripped too tightly on her breasts, pinching them instead of caressing. She groaned in pain and he heard her groan. Maggie liked that.

***

Back behind the red door of the little house just south of the Texas border, the old woman who had served Maggie eggs told her to make sure she had lots of water. She told her to look out for Lupe, who the old woman knew was weak. She told her to keep her head down and not speak unless spoken to. She told her to find her people in the States and never leave them. Then the old woman patted her on the head as if Maggie was a dog and she said that she felt only good things would come of this, that Maggie was destined to cross and cross easily.

Then the old lady crossed herself and Maggie felt obliged to do the same.

"You say this to everyone," Maggie said as she finished with the Holy Ghost.

The old woman shrugged and told her to finish her milk.

***

William had done this before but now, here, the girls' eyes were too bright for him. They were too eager. They were all so young.

If he were a different man, a completely different kind of man, he would choose one and take her into the small back room that smelled of knock-off perfume and bug spray, mime the words of Dylan Thomas or Luis Borges, and fall in love in a crumpled mess on stained sheets.

But he was the same man he always was and, as he looked at the lineup, all he could see were girls on the verge of womanhood who were waiting to die. Like little caged African greys.

He felt sick, a deep nausea coming from the pit of his stomach. He excused himself but had no idea how to leave.

"*El baño está aquel,*" the madam said, bored. She pointed to the far corner.

William went where she pointed and, once in the small bathroom, planned his escape.

***

Maggie and Lupe left just as dusk fell. They were fifteen years old. Almost sixteen, Maggie might have corrected. Their hips were still boyish and slim and they were simply too young to understand what awaited them. The man who was taking them across the border was named Guillermo, but he asked to be called Guam. He sniffed at nothing.

"I'm an island in the middle of nowhere, belonging to no one."

Maggie thought he was handsome but too nervous, his face unshaved, with the spotty beard of a young man not fully grown. He was Mexican but also American.

'He does belong nowhere,' Maggie thought.

"I fucking hate this gig," he said. Maggie, so young, found his indifference sexy but knew better than to let him know this.

The day wore on, and with it, the mystery of Guam, the appeal of his nowhere-ness and isolation, waned into annoyance and even to the fringe of dislike. When they were five miles into their hike, he made them stop and check their bags. He had done the exact same thing when they were just outside the red door, then again in the small village that smelled of slain animals, chicken, pork, goat, then again in the outlying ranches and now in the desert, where the heat gave way to the rippling illusion of just out-of-reach liquid.

Maggie wanted to say something in protest, but kept silent. Guam put his finger up to test for wind direction. Maggie dropped the forty-five pound shell she carried on her back and looked through it, searching for the items Guam wanted to make sure were present. Inertia was winning. Both the girls wanted to leave the bags lying there on the sand and gravel. Instead, they dutifully lifted each item to show it was present and accounted for.

"Good girls. Now, onward." The bags would be lifted, slower and with more resistance each time.

"Keep up *meijas*, keep up," he would say as they trudged on, and then he would sprint ahead of them, sometimes howling at some unseen wolf.

Finally, Maggie couldn't see any of the lights from the village behind her. Nothing north to the United States, either. She, too, she had become an island.

Maggie and Lupe tried not to make eye contact as they walked a few paces behind the howling Guam. If they did, they might both burst into tears.

"Check your bags for flashlights." He said stopping them again. Maggie had sweat through her white T-shirt. "We just did that," she said.

"Do it again. And those protein bars and tape and water. Gotta have water at all times."

"Where would the water have gone since the last time we checked for it?"

Guam didn't answer her.

So they did as they were told, even though Maggie knew they might miss their rendezvous point with all this stopping and checking.

"It will be okay," she muttered to Lupe and she hoped she was telling the truth.

***

Sal rubbed Maggie's back.

"Are you good?" Sal asked.

"I'm perfect."

"You seem distant."

Sal grabbed Maggie's face and held it in his hand. She could feel the calloused fingertips grip her jaw.

"I've got condoms back at my place," Sal said. Maggie could see his erection through his jeans.

"I'm on the pill." Then she leaned over and rubbed him hard.

"I've heard that before," he said, and stopped her advances. "Is this is your attempt to get me to marry you?" he asked.

"Shut up and get to work."

She undid the seatbelt and slid her body over and on top of him.

***

William wriggled his way out of the small window above a dirty shower. Sweat poured down his brow and made ringlets on his shirt. His chest heaved up and down.

He closed his eyes and thought of the last time he had paid for it. It was Downtown. He had studied the subway stations for hours online. He knew to get off near Flower and head west three blocks. The woman had called herself Callie; she lived in a loft space, though he wasn't sure what that meant. He could see in her pictures online the San Gabriel Mountains behind her large breasts and leather corset. Everything about that excited him.

He buzzed the apartment number she had told him to buzz and when he went inside, a doorman asked him to sign his name. Somehow, over time, his signature had become his father's. The W looped way up like a lasso and the rest was a mess of squiggles, a Richter scale of a John Hancock.

She had the door open before he knocked. She was bigger than her picture, full figured, like the women in the Sears catalogues he took to the bathroom when he was an adolescent. He liked that.

"They stay snow-capped almost the entire year," he remembered her saying about the mountains in the distance.

He paid her the money up front and then they had sex on her sofa. It was awkward, but he was grateful she at least looked him in the eyes, upon every thrust, her pale blue eyes, drowning in black smear.

He had done this before, and successfully, so why did he want to vomit? Go back in there and do this like you did Callie, he told himself. He tried to trumpet his nerve into returning to the row of girls, but he couldn't move. He rested against the crumbling wall immersed with graffiti commenting on the power of the Chupacabra.

And then he heard something from down the alley. He lifted his head and his breathing calmed.

It was a woman singing:

> *El lobo rabíoso*
> *La quiso morder*
> *Mas Díos poderso*
> *La supó defender.*

William was shocked by the paucity of talent in the woman's voice. Her tone was horrendous. Her pitch was uneven and woeful. But the sheer commitment to the words, to the phrasing, forced him to go to where the voice emanated. He walked down the dingy alley, past a drunk man pissing, past a bored tabby too sick to fight, past promises made in freshly poured cement years and years ago. Jesus might save and Omar might love Vera forever but tonight all was decayed except for the big red moon and this voice of the lobos, both of which hung precarious and low in the Mexican sky.

"Don't go to her," the man who pissed said as he zipped up his pants. "Stay out here old man and buy me a beer. I know where we can get some for fifteen pesetas."

William walked away from the drunken man and his offer.

"Don't say I didn't warn you," the drunken man yelled.

William followed the voice to a vent. Shards of lint flitted through the cage-like opening but didn't blow out. A spider carcass was rolled up in the ball in one corner, a curious bookend to the dead dragonfly rolled up in the dead spider's web.

Under the vent was a door. He turned the rusted knob and was surprised to find the door open. He let himself in.

***

Sal fell asleep quickly. Maggie rested her head awkwardly on his shoulder. The center console was digging into the small of her back but she was afraid to move. She didn't want to wake him up. This was her favorite part, when it was over but not finished.

His breathing was already deep and she could see his eyes moving rapidly beneath his eyelids.

She could never date someone like Sal. He was too big, too archetypal. He belonged in a bar somewhere in Mexico. And Fresno was the only place men like Sal should ever be from. He was good for a night, maybe for breakfast the next day, but she could never bring him north to visit Lupe in San Francisco. This man was old enough to be her father, maybe, with this white hair receding too rapidly for pills or aerosol spray, his careless belly bursting from his waist.

She tried to wrap her arms all the way around it. She let her fingers slide off his left leg and she felt something in between his leg and the door. It was a gun. She could feel the cold metallic thickness of the handle.

This wasn't the first time she had felt a gun. And like the other times, she was both afraid and comforted.

She let go of the handle and nestled onto his heaving chest. The center console continued to dig into the small of her back as she closed her eyes and waited for sleep.

***

"Don't go anywhere. Wait here behind this rock." Guam was speaking in shorter sentences now, five hours into their sojourn.

"Why, Guam?" Maggie said. The desire to giggle had ceased. Guam's paranoia had rubbed off on her. She too was hearing noises in the silent desert. Lupe clung to her and she clung back, holding her favorite Lupe doll as tightly as she could.

"Because. Because it might be the only safe place out here. Black helicopters are everywhere. They fly low and sound like owls. We can never be too sure. Those owls hunt and kill. Big claws that reach down from the sky and once they dig into you, they don't let go. We are the fucking mice. They are clawed and vicious and then we spend time getting deported and all this money and time is fucking wasted. So wait here. Behind this rock."

The girls did as they were told. Guam checked his bag yet again.

"This is why you paid me," he said after he was done searching for whatever he was searching for. "I'll be back. Promise."

"Let's pray," Lupe said.

"Ssssh. Lupe. Just be quiet."

***

William followed the singing through the door and down a hall made of tin. The woman's clumsy warbling echoed loudly off the corrugated edifice. The hall led to a large foyer of sorts, with a cracked mirror directly opposite the entrance William stood in. Overhead, a single light bulb hung from where a chandelier once was. Some invisible current of air swayed the light bulb to and fro. William's shadow danced around the room.

The singing came to an abrupt stop.

"Ricardo? Is that you?" Her voice retained a singsong quality and it had a fuzzy sound to it, like a child speaking into an oscillating fan.

William shook his head.

"Ricardo, come in *mi todo*, please. Come in."

William took a step toward the open door next to the mirror.

"Se da prisa, amor."

He reached the doorway and peered in. The room was lit only by candles but there were scores of them. Lit on top of shelves, chairs, the floor. Books lay flat and candles sat upon them. The small window in the corner had a dozen on its molded sill.

"Come and sit by me. I've been waiting all day for you."

William shuffled into the room. How odd, he thought. In the middle of a room was a Victorian-style, four-post bed. It smelled of mildew and he could hear water dripping from some unseen leak in the roof.

He found the wolf singer on her back. She kicked her legs up when she realized he had entered the room.

"Come closer, Ricardo. Why are you playing coy, today?"

William wondered who Ricardo was and then he forgot all about him. She was wearing a silk slip and nothing else. Her breasts were exposed and

large and her belly was taut and flat. And she was
older, a woman, not a girl. She had dancer's legs and
pointed her arched feet to the ceiling.

William thought she was the most beautiful
creature he had ever seen.

Then, as he neared her, through the
candlelight, he saw her more closely. Her hands
were tied up and tethered to the posts of the bed.
Her long hair went well past her waist and her eyes
were blindfolded. She was being held captive.

"Don't look so surprised, Ricardo. These are
your chains. Now, why don't you be a prince and
help me out."

***

It was cold in the car. Maggie thought she might
go and look for William. It had been almost forty-
five minutes. But she didn't. She reached over and
flipped the ignition key so that she could turn on the
heater. The commotion startled Sal awake.

"Go back to sleep, Sal. I was just cold."

"Where's the old guy?"

"Still gone."

"Good for him."

Then he shut his eyes and went back to sleep.

Maggie waited for the warm air to pass through
the vents, holding her hands against the slatted
openings.

***

Lupe was stroking Maggie's hair when she finally awoke. It was six, maybe six thirty in the morning.

"We're still alive."

Yes, thought Maggie. They were.

"Let's go," Maggie said.

"Where? We should stay here and wait for him." Lupe said.

"No. He's not coming for us. Let's get up and walk."

"Where?"

"North. Let's not sit here and wait for the wolves to come."

"We can go back. Maybe we should go back."

"I'm not going back ever. Come on, Lupe." Maggie reached down and helped Lupe off the dusty desert ground. Each wiped the dirt from their jeans.

"Check your bag for water." Maggie said. Lupe managed a smile. Then they left the shadow of the rock and moved north. They were already in Texas, that great state of very big things.

***

Sal was Monster, who was the guy that night after the bar, who was the boy with long hair like a woman's, who was Freddy, the king of victimology, who was the rockabilly poet who had that cowlick that he said was born the day his father beat him too hard, who was Ricky the gangbanger who tattooed Maggie drunk on three forties of malt liquor, who was Jerry her first Asian, who was that kid who kept his headshot on him, ("success is when luck meets preparedness," he told her). Before that she forgot the names, the places they'd fucked, but each one was the same so none of it mattered anyway.

Maggie leaned against the hood of the car and smoked a cigarette she'd stolen from Sal's breast pocket. She hadn't smoked regularly since Alan, her gay husband. Drunk on the patio of his Silverlake home, nothing was better than watching the Dodger traffic inch down Sunset on an August night. Songs from radios wafting in the air, four chords of delights.

"You'll never have a relationship with any man longer than the one you've had with me," Alan said, handing her a lit smoke.

"Not true," she said. "Plus, you're not really a man."

"Fuck you."

"I love you, too, Alan."

***

William sat down on the bed next to the captive, half-naked woman.

"It's over there," she waved her hand in the direction of a small table. "Bring some to me."

William didn't move. He looked at her breasts. They were terror-inducing and riveting and everything William had ever wanted.

"Ricardo, please. I need a little bit more." She lifted her legs up and repositioned them in William's lap.

"Ricardo?" she said. The singsong quality was gone. She tried to sit up too abruptly, forgetting she was chained. Her body jerked back to where it had been. "Who the fuck is there? Where the hell is Ricardo?"

William stood up quickly, knocking her legs off of his lap. He squeaked and tried to catch her legs but they fell hard on the mattress.

"I swear to God, whoever this is, get out of here." She waited. William didn't move.

"Are you here to hurt me?"

William shook his head no.

"I'll take your silence as a no. How did you find me?"

William shrugged.

"Do me a favor. Come towards me and take off my mask." Her voice had become seductive again.

William did as she asked. He gently reached behind her neck and released the strings that were knotted there. The black mask fell away from her eyes. She blinked a few times and then wet her lips. Strands of hair clung to her face, glued by sweat. William took his sleeve and dabbed her brow.

"Thank you," she said.

William dropped his head.

"Look up at me. A gringo with a sad face. What a wonderful surprise. Do you speak Spanish?"

William nodded.

"Good. I find English tiresome. The Italian in me likes the romance of Spanish. Now. Go to that drawer please."

William walked to the drawer.

"Good. Now use that key to scoop up some of that powder there. Good. Good. Bring it to me and place it under my nose."

William did as he was told. She took a long sniff and the powder disappeared up her nostril.

"Isn't that just the sexiest thing?" She laughed. "I should tell you first that I have never believed in anything and feel all the lighter because of it." She closed her eyes and hummed a few bars of the song she was singing earlier. William could see all the way up her slip. He tried his best not to look. He failed.

"So, what brings you to my small room in the middle of nowhere?" Her wrists twisted in their cuffs. "Here to find yourself? Take some time off from the fast lane of American life? I think many things about America. How can you not? But it's foolish to believe in America and it's foolish to believe against America. It's just a mass of land with people. It's not good nor is it evil. Don't think too much about America. Like all of us, it too is dying."

William, for once, was glad he was speechless.

"I lived there for many years. But the thing was, all I wanted to do was just stay in the house. Never leave my room. It's the safest thing to do, but then nothing will get done. Nothing will be built. I am talking about infrastructure. That's what won't get done if we all stay in our rooms. It's a dilemma. I am talking about building society from the ground up. Where did all the carpenters go? Where did all the masons and the cement mixers go? They went to Mexico and this is why I am here. To give encouragement to those that build. I moved here to take communion with the builders and stay in my little room for as long as I like."

She rubbed her legs together like a cricket. William knew the drugs had kicked in.

"Ricardo will be here soon and he might kill you if he finds you here. He is big and has the temper of an angry wasp. He stings with little cause and less remorse. I've seen him crush men for having foul breath."

William turned around, expecting to find Ricardo in the doorway, but no one was there.

"Don't be afraid, my pet," the woman said, laughing. "Remember, we all have to die. Now, I would like a kiss from you. Every girl dreams of a kiss from a rich white man. Come here and kiss me, just one time."

She closed her eyes and puckered her lips. William thought he heard a door open. He froze for a second and then bolted for the door.

When he got outside, he stopped. He wanted to kiss her. He wanted to kiss her so badly it hurt him, pangs shot up his legs and down his arms. There was no noise. Plus, she was high and obviously touched. He told himself that Ricardo didn't even exist.

He turned around and marched back into her room. He sat down on the edge of her bed, bent his face toward her and kissed her, using one hand to caress the back of her neck, and his other hand to reach beneath her pink slip.

She melted into him.

Then, just as quickly, she pulled her face away from William's. A siren's moan escaped the corner of her mouth and her eyes widened.

"He's here. Ricardo," she said in a whisper. William could smell the man, anise and bourbon, without even turning to look.

***

Maggie and Lupe finally stumbled across a bit of good fortune. With only one more liter of water between them and well after they had eaten their last morsel of food, a pickup truck with a camper shell drove up beside them as they wandered like lost camels in the intense heat of the two o'clock sun.

The driver, an older white man with a ten-gallon hat, rolled down his window and stopped the truck.

"What the hell are you two doing out here?"

Maggie told him what had happened, as best she could, in the few words of English she knew.

"Get in," he said. The girls went to the back of the truck. "Wait. You," he said, pointing at Maggie, "You come up front with me. You look white. Or white enough. Pass as my wife. It'll make it easier."

Then he opened the back of the camper shell and helped Lupe into it. Inside, twenty-five others were laying silently in the back, one on top of the other, a human pyramid.

"Climb inside," the man ordered. Maggie nudged Lupe forward. The man went back up to the front of the trunk. You'll be fine, Maggie wanted to say. But she didn't. Lupe climbed up on the fender and then disappeared inside the camper. A couple of groans could be heard, but the fear of noise quelled any unnecessary sound. The groans were replaced by an eerie silence, a silence that shouldn't be present when that many humans were in such a small space.

Maggie closed the camper shell door and twisted the handle shut. She could see through the tinted window as Lupe pressed her body against the body below her. Her back was pushed hard against the roof of the camper. Those bruises would last for weeks.

Maggie felt the dry Texas wind blow through her hair and she tried her best not to like it. But she did. She closed her eyes and it let it whip her hair around, a dervish of course, black twisters. The driver laughed and blasted the radio. It was music that Maggie had never heard before, but she loved it. She loved everything.

It was done in a gas station bathroom, after they had left El Paso, while the human blankets sweated in silence in the back of the camper, still afraid of any noise that might arouse suspicion from some unseen border cop. Maggie was noiseless as well, bent over the dirty toilet. She closed her eyes and thought of that old woman in the house with the big red door. She remembered the woman patting her head like a dog and telling her that she would be okay, that she was destined to cross safely. I look like I could be his wife, Maggie told herself.

On the ground, someone had left a magazine and Maggie tried to read the English words but she couldn't. She tried with all her might but she just couldn't figure out what it said.

***

Sal and Maggie were both awake now. A cloud obscured the moon and for a moment the sky was dark.

"Let's just go back to my place," Sal said. "He's probably asleep. Antoñia will take care of him for the night." He leaned on the hood next to Maggie. He yawned, still waking up from his nap.

"Antoñia is the madam lady?"

Sal nodded.

"And you're sure he'll be okay?"

"He's a grown man, Maggie. Let him have some fun."

"Okay. We'll pick him up first thing tomorrow."

"That nap gave me just what I need for round two," Sal said and draped his arms over Maggie. She leaned back into him as he sat on the hood of his car.

Then she tugged at Sal's hand, indicating it was time to go home, if only for the night.

18

William could speak. His throat felt of velvet. He stood out on the edge of a natural ridge and viewed the crowd that had gathered in the valley. In the background, a ring of minor hills and sharp buttes encircled them. William raised his hands and a hush fell over the people there. The crowd was made up of ghosts: opaque, invisible, barely there, ferocious, bitter, sullen specters of various sizes and shapes. William didn't notice they were dead, or if he did, he didn't care. His voice came out strong and slightly raspy like loose gravel:

"What happens when nothing happens, despite a risk? What happens when disconnection is all you've ever had and all you ever will have? What happens when you realize that your timeline has expired?" William paused for effect. It worked. The crowd of phantoms squeezed tighter together, waiting on his next thought.

"Do you fight it?"

The crowd gasped as a collective.

"Accept it?"

The crowd turned to each other and wondered what the answer might be.

"What does that acceptance look like? What happens when you realize the rest of your life is void of magic?"

He was a mighty rhetorical pastor, talking to his flock of dead. His sermon wasn't on a mount, but a dry lakebed that seemingly stretched forever. Tufts of cloud dotted the sky. Dogbane and Spanish Needle broke the brown monotony as cracks bled along the bottom of the dead lake and the grooves dug so deep, that some of the ghosts fell in between them and never came back.

"I couldn't speak once. Believe it or not, I was made silent by the hard Ds and confounding As of the English language. And those softer middle-accented sounds so common in Spanish. All of those twenty-six consonants and vowels vexed me. Got the better of me. And I began a great depression that would last sixty odd years. I waited for magic and it never came. I began to believe that I was nothing more than a broken wheel on a rundown wagon. And it was when I was at my lowest, when even the hint of magic was nowhere to be seen that I began to..."

William paused here. He knew what he had to say next. He had practiced it over and over. This was when the sermon turned from dire to redemptive. He knew how it ended. He cleared his throat. The sun was shining but it wasn't hot. The cool breeze seemed to annoy the ghosts.

His throat tensed. The words were stuck inside, like the ghosts trapped in the cracks. He smiled and laughed. His cheeks flushed.

The ghosts began to murmur. It sounded like a feeble wind through a row of junipers. The feeling of dissent was palpable. William remained speechless. Some of the ghosts began to leave. They flew skyward, great balloons of flimsy almost-beings. Then more joined them in the exodus. William beckoned them to stay, but they ignored him. He ran down the ridge, trying to grab onto any of the last remaining ghosts, but each slipped through his fingers. The ghosts were all gone and William stood alone on the dry lakebed coughing up sounds.

"Wake up, *abuelo*," the man called Ricardo said. William felt a shooting pain in his temple. He couldn't see anything. His hand instinctually went to touch the spot where the pain throbbed but the man called Ricardo batted it down with one strong swat. William could feel dried blood on the nape of his neck. The blood cracked when he twisted.

The air in the truck was more than briny, heavier than salt. It made William nauseous but he kept himself in check.

"You don't kiss another hombre's woman, old man."

William blinked over and over but his swollen eyes wouldn't open. He couldn't remember kissing anyone. He felt around, trying to remember where he was and how he had gotten there. He heard the loud blow of a semi's horn and knew he was on the road. Then he rested his head upon some kind of cushion and passed out cold.

19

"Thought you might want something to eat," Sal said, handing Maggie a cup of coffee and stirring some oatmeal in a large black pot.

"Yeah. Sure."

She was timid in the sunshine. So was he. He stirred the pot recklessly, but with precision. His eyes never left the oats. She wanted to ask for cream and one more sugar, but didn't. The coffee burned the back of her throat as he poured the breakfast into a plastic bowl.

"You, find the, uh, floss and toothpaste okay?"

"Yeah, it was under the sink. Just like you said."

"Of course it was. I put it there. Well, you eat up, I have to run a quick errand and then we'll head out and find old Playboy Willie."

Maggie was glad when he left. She pretended to read the paper he had out on the table, but she just stared at the black and white words until they blurred like specks of dirt in a flurry of snow. The vicissitudes of the local wayfarer, the damage done by a disgraced politician, the fall of a foreign market, the drug mules and drug deaths and drug stings were all fodder for the trash liner. She found more sugar on the counter next to the pot of oatmeal and put in three lumps. She stirred the coffee and thought of sex with Sal, the sugar swirling and swirling until finally the coffee was palatable.

William trembled, he was afraid to open his eyes. He sat as rigid as possible to counteract the shaking of his limbs. Finally, he let his hands roam, searching with curious fingers to figure out where he was. He was sitting on concrete. He could smell other men around him, musky and stale, the smell of trapped men.

He opened his eyes. The light was minimal, but there was enough of it and he could see where he was. He was in a small jail. A police officer or a secretary or someone was resting his head on a desk on the other side of the metal bars. William wondered if that was Ricardo.

His head was throbbing. He twisted his neck, trying to alleviate the pain. It only made the pain worse.

"Hey there, cowboy," the man next to him said in Spanish. William nodded. The man looked away.

There were seven other men in with him, each drunk, half shirtless, most shoeless. It scared him to breathe. Suddenly the man on the other side of William stood up. He stretched his arms and shook out his legs. He had a wicked smile on his face. He reached down his pants and pulled out a small bottle of gin, downing its contents. Then he began to twirl around, dancing to some invisible waltz with the ghost of a woman. His worn tennis shoes splashed the stagnant urine that made lakes and rivers in the uneven concrete floor. The man began to mutter words in English, a song William assumed he made up on the spot.

"It's only when you've been caged, that you live to run," he sang, as he twirled faster, tossing around his invisible woman with great speed. For a moment, William saw her, the invisible woman, in a ball gown of some shiny material, a southern Belle, maybe, with a flower on her wrist, a white one with a pink center. She had that unbridled look of joy that befalls women when they've been asked to dance a waltz.

"It's only when you've lived in shit that you can truly see the sun." The man was dancing so rapidly, almost violently, that he was nearly out of breath and the last of his lyrics were barely audible.

"Shut the fuck up you *pinché puta*," said another prisoner.

But the man didn't shut up. He kept his dancing and found a new, steadier rhythm. His balance was stronger than when he had started his little number.

"It's only when the puta is long gone, that you ever learn to cum."

Two men laughed at this and William realized they all were awake, despite their silence.

Then the man lost his balance and fell down.

"Shut the fuck up in there, you Nicaraguan piece of shit." the officer said without lifting his head. "Go the fuck back to sleep."

The man crawled back to his seat next to William. William shut his eyes and tried to fall back asleep.

If he had had the strength, he would have gotten up from the concrete slab and offered his arm to the invisible woman and helped her up. Then, with her safely in his arms, he would have danced with her for hours and hours, until his own legs collapsed.

But there was no woman, only a tank of drunk, crazy men locked away for the night as coyotes bayed somewhere in the flat desert with its black, twinkling sky.

20

Maggie smoked another cigarette as she waited for Sal. Her cell phone rang. It was her mother.

Fuck. She kicked a rock. She let it go to voicemail.

Sal walked down the small path from the red door to the car.

"He wasn't here last night."

"What do you mean?"

"Antoñia said he stayed only for a few minutes, then left."

"What the fuck do you mean?"

"He's not here and I don't know where he is."

"Fuck. Fuck. I have to go and get my mother. We were supposed to be there today. Fuck."

"We'll find him. There aren't that many places he can be."

They retraced their steps from the previous night. They went back to where they had dropped off William near Antoñia's, asked the drunk man if he had seen him (he hadn't, but he might be able to find out just where he was for a few pesetas), went back to Sal's bar to see if he might have found his way there. They drove around the small downtown, looked behind a few dumpsters. Sal called a few women he knew. William wasn't anywhere.

"Well, he's either dead or in jail," Sal said.

Maggie took another drag of her cigarette. The day had heated up and she rolled down the window of Sal's truck. Then she put her feet on the dash.

"That's dangerous," Sal said. He brushed her feet off.

"I feel like living dangerously," Maggie said.

"We should get some money."

"Why?"

"I don't think William's dead."

It went smoothly. Sal had done this before, Maggie could tell. He took the money she had withdrawn from an ATM then he walked into the office of the jail and started chatting up the officer. She followed him, staying a few steps behind. She saw William, as Sal and the guard talked town gossip, a little soccer.

"Damn," she said quietly.

Sal pointed to William. The man said someone had dropped William off in the middle of the night. Sal put three hundred dollar bills in the man's hand. William was released five minutes later.

Sal used his hand to guide William towards the truck.

Maggie kept her distance from the men, a few feet behind.

"Looks like you had quite a night," Maggie said as Sal helped William along. "It's only gonna cost you three hundred dollars."

William nodded.

He stared straight ahead as he shuffled along, his feet barely lifting off the ground. He pretended he was back home, eating peaches and having a pinch of whiskey. His eyes burned. His throat felt sore and raspy.

"So, where the hell did you go?" Maggie asked.

William shrugged.

"Can't fucking shrug everything away. You can't do that. Where the hell did you go and why the fuck do you look like a battered wife?"

William didn't shrug.

They all got into Sal's car.

"I feel like I have a child on my hands. A willful, stupid child who doesn't know how to behave himself. It's ridiculous."

"Maggie," said Sal.

"Just drive. We have to get going."

Sal asked for Maggie's number. He asked if they would ever see each other again. "Probably not," Maggie told him, but she gave him her number anyway. Sal said he would try and get to Los Angeles sometime soon and Maggie kissed him on the cheek.

"Be safe," Sal told William. They shook hands.

21

They drove fast down the highway. Maggie was silent. A piece of the fabric from the ceiling of the van had fallen down and rustled like a sail in the wind from her open window.

William was fine to just stare out at the desert.

They ate at a Hercules. The place had tables that reminded William of lawn furniture. The Coke machine was coughing and sputtering but the young woman behind the counter didn't seem bothered by the noise. The menu, hanging above her, was handwritten in a rainbow of different colors and each menu items seemed to have been written by a different person.

Maggie kept her silence. In line, she stayed a constant three feet away from him. When she placed her order she didn't ask him what he wanted. She ordered a fried chicken torta with onion rings for herself and then sat down at the table, leaving William standing in line.

He knew that she wanted him to tell her what happened, but he couldn't, even if he had a voice that worked. He couldn't tell her that he just wanted to kiss a woman. A real woman that he didn't have to pay for, that didn't feel sorry for him. The Wolf Singer had wanted him. She asked him for a kiss. In what language could he possibly explain how that felt to Maggie?

"What can I get for you?" The lady said.

William looked at the menu. He was starving. She asked him again what he wanted. He turned around, but Maggie was staring out the window.

"Sir?"

William started to breathe heavy.

"Sir?"

Two men behind him were arguing over who was going to pay.

"Sir?"

The men's voices were getting louder and louder. Each insisted it was the other's turn to pay.

"Sir?" She raised her voice to overcome the loudness of the men.

William pointed to the board.

"The torta with onion rings?"

William nodded.

She shook her head and William gave her a twenty in American money.

As William waited for his food, the lady behind the counter waited for the victor of the yelling men. She drummed her fingers, painted bright orange to match the décor, looking at William while she did and then took the money from the man who'd lost.

Another worker dinged a bell and William grabbed the tray of food meant for him and shuffled back to Maggie and their table.

As he ate his meal with slow, deliberate bites, William began to feel as though his fingers were shrinking.

He stretched them to make sure they weren't.

Then the torta seemed to get bigger.

William glanced around to see if anyone else saw what he was seeing. No one seemed to. He took another bite.

But then his fingers began to contract and the weight of the meat and the bread fast became too big a burden and he set the thing down in the plastic tray, the top piece of bread falling over, exposing a glop of mayonnaise under a dislodged tomato.

He sat still, Sunday-morning-church still, as he watched his fingers begin to disappear. He attempted to feel, to qualify, to understand this sudden change. It had to be there, in some corporeal cavity. It, this amendment in his structure, this hallucination of proportion, must be present at the cellular level, he reasoned silently to himself as Maggie slurped her soda, maybe just below the surface of the skin, maybe in that place on the back of one's throat that gets tickled and sore. He closed his eyes and searched for it. For the feeling of his shrinking fingers. But nothing was there. He felt exactly the same as he had yesterday, as he had all his life.

Maybe it was an accident, he thought. An odd mistake that just happened, the way things happen, the way pets die. But this was happening to him and not just to his fingers. Each of his limbs was folding in on itself.

He yelled at Maggie to save him but she couldn't hear. She was chewing her food slowly, a sated predator.

And then, suddenly, he realized what it was:

He was six years old and the speech pathologist told him if he sang the words they would come out fluently.

So he had tried to sing the words but no melody was heard.

He was six years old and he wanted to tell Kathy Drudger he loved her, that he loved her purple barrettes and pigtails that were never quite even, but he couldn't say a word and she told him he had a stupid grin and a bad haircut and then ran to play on the swing set.

He was twelve and a junior high basketball coach told him he needed to practice speech like he did free throws. Repetition, over and over, studying what he did right and repeating, studying what he did wrong and discarding that.

So he did that and it yielded nothing but wasted hours in front of the mirror, watching his mouth twist into caricature. Later, he bought himself a voice recorder, but that failed, too.

He was thirteen and as the acne rose from his cheeks like great Mayan temples, he watched Betty Grains' breasts grow right in front of him. This excited him to his very core, to a place of spiritual devotion but he knew that he would never feel them, or her, and so he learned to never look at her newly developed breasts, but instead find a spot on the ground and look there instead.

"A cup for every saucer," his mom told him at fifteen. "You'll find the right girl, a girl who doesn't care you're a mute. A girl who likes the fact you're a mute. Now, go tell your father to come down. Pork chops tonight."

So he waited year after year, always remembering what his mother had told him, always believing that his saucer was out there.

His mother was a liar.

(He tried to pick up the sandwich again, but shrunken arms made the task impossible. They looked like broken limbs from a backyard lemon tree, made sick with blight.)

His father rarely spoke to him, even though his father had no trouble speaking.

"He loves you, William, you're just a little strange to him is all," his mother said when he was eighteen and graduating from high school. "Just wait until college. You'll find what you're supposed to do. He'll be proud of you then. Trust me."

But William never went to college. He came back from the state school, the only school that accepted him, after three weeks. His dorm mate had given him myriad uninteresting nicknames involving Williams from history and television (William the Stammerer, Billy the KKKid, William Shitner). In the dining hall, he sat alone eating sticky rice and ice cream sundaes. His professors ignored him. Women avoided him. He was worse than a pariah. He was invisible.

"Learn a trade," his brother had told him when he was twenty-one. "One that you don't need to speak to get the job done."

This advice William utilized. He learned the trade of janitor and this was how he lived for the next four decades of his life. His legacy was toilets and Sisyphean efforts of erasing bathroom poetry and blowjob phone numbers.

(William tried to reach for an onion ring but his shoulder was shriveled and dried. He looked at it, atrophied, diseased, and had to close his eyes)

William was sixty years old, standing in front of a counter woman, wanting to order a burger but stuck eating a torta instead.

The truth was, William was shrinking. He was becoming the smallest man alive, he was a receding empire watching all of its territory erode into ruin and neglect. He had nothing to go back to. His friends were dead. Ricardo was right. One never kisses another man's woman. So he would never kiss again. He sat in his corner of a pastel-colored booth as Maggie ignored him and he was, for the first time, void of even the tiniest drop of the smallest sample of hope.

For the first time in his life, William wanted to die.

He looked at his fingers and hands. They were perfectly normal.

He scooted his body off the pastel bench, his face still stinging from Ricardo's punch and walked out of the Hercules, leaving his half eaten meal on the table.

Fifteen minutes later, Maggie came out to the van. William was standing by the passenger-side door watching the sky. Not saying a word, she got into the driver's side, reached over to unlock his door, started the car and drove away before he'd even had the chance to settle in.

An hour later his finger was on the car door handle. He thought if he opened it, he could just roll himself out and smash onto the concrete. Pedro and Sammy and all those dreams he'd had seemed to foreshadow this event. Dead on the hot Mexican asphalt highway. His breath came quickly. He undid his seatbelt. Maggie didn't notice. She was driving in the left lane. He looked over his shoulder to make sure there were cars in the right lane. He wanted to be thorough. He asked Jesus' forgiveness, just to be safe. Then he fiddled the door handle.

He saw himself opening it then thrusting his body away from the seat and onto the road, a post-industrial river. His body would hit the ground, smack it hard, pebbles instantly embedding in skin, rendering him unconscious. Then he would roll over and over, the cars behind the van would run him over, smashing bone and sinew, shredding his skin, flattening his organs. Long after he was gone, floating in the light or the darkness, his body would have to deal with more cars, more rubber, more chrome.

His fingers wrapped around the handle. He wanted to pull it. He made sure it was unlocked. It was. He looked over at Maggie. She would see him in her rearview, limp and torn and pummeled. She would see him. He let his fingers fall from the metal handle. He couldn't let her see him.

It was wrong, he reasoned, to even think about doing it with her in the car. It could wait. What was another hour or day in a lifetime of dead hours and dead days?

He leaned back in the seat and looked outside at the desert its watery lines of confusion snaking around the horizon.

He could feel the heat even though the window was closed, the door was locked and the air conditioner blasted out coolness.

"Here," Maggie said. "Got you a soda."

She had stopped off for a bathroom break. William hardly even noticed but took the drink and nodded gratefully.

They were climbing the Sierra Madres now, the van seeming to inch along.

"I remember once when I was a kid," Maggie mused, "my father got ripped drunk after a cousin's first communion. I mean, ripped. My best friend Lupe was staying over that night. We were up late, telling ghost stories or whatever. In walks my dad from his bedroom. No shirt on. His eyes are bright red. Like tail lights. He walks, well, stumbles, to the potted plant and starts pissing in it." Maggie laughed. "So damn funny."

Against a jutting butte, a large red tailed hawk circled the sky, surveying the decay.

"I was worried about you. That's all."

William nodded.

"And I want to turn this van around so bad it fucking hurts. I want to go home and get back to my life."

William reached over and squeezed her hand. She let him. Then he let her hand go and gazed out the window, not looking for anything in particular.

Soon night was falling and William had never in his life seen the sky so lit up by stars.

As they neared Juárez, the radio picked up more stations.

"Thank god," Maggie said when she found a Texas rock station. "Any more ranchero music and I would have killed myself."

They came down a small hill and the initial lights of the sprawling city blinked before them. A large field of pink crosses came into view in a desolate field.

"They look like broken windmills or potted plants that grew too large to tend to," Maggie said.

They did, thought William. That's exactly what they looked like. Either of her examples.

Maggie took out her phone.

"Hey, Lupe."

Maggie put the phone on speaker and placed her phone on her knee so she could listen and drive.

"No, we had to come up to Juarez to pick up Mama."

"Sotera bolted for the States I guess. Mama tried to chase her down. Took us a whole day out of our way but I had to do it."

"The city? It looks the same I guess." Maggie's voice dropped. "It's night. Can't see much."

But William saw much. The dollar exchange stores and the large metal bars that protected those inside. The empty restaurants and the wide streets where traffic should have been. A woman holding her young baby close to her chest, waiting for the light to change.

"So how are you?" She asked with a bit too much pep.

"Good, good." Lupe volleyed back greetings.

"Good. It's good."

"Are you going out tonight? Dancing, drinking?"

They whirred down Calle Vicente Guerrero, past the Cathedral, past the Benito Juarez monument, purple and glorious in the brazen late-summer air.

"I don't care if you're married. I don't care if you're tired. I want you and Ernesto to go out tonight. Go out and dance, chica."

"Promise?"

"Okay. Love you. I'll call you soon."

"Besos." Maggie ended the call and threw the phone in the center console.

The city was a mess of ideas, houses and cars. It reminded William of Los Angeles. Spread out, thick with the bluster of buildings. The stars had all been extinguished by man-made light.

Finally, Maggie looked at William.

"Here we are," she said.

22

William held up the map.

"Find Calle de Perros," Maggie said. "Her motel is on that street."

William stared at the map ineffectually.

"William, what is wrong with you? We're friends again. I am nothing if not forgiving. Now, help me out."

William found the street and pointed where to turn. Then he let the map slip from his fingers and drop to the floor. After twenty minutes of navigating the nearly empty streets, Maggie found the little motel on the corner. She eased the van into a parking spot. The gravel was loose like birdseed. She picked up her phone and called.

"No answer." Maggie was fidgeting. She was nervous.

"Let's get out and look for her. Maybe she's eating or at the pool. Ha! As if this is the fucking Four Seasons."

They walked around the small grounds to no avail. Maggie then went to the front desk to ask for help.

"Front desk clerk says she's in room 19. Let's go check there first." Maggie said when she returned to the van. William was fixated on a man across the street changing his tire. The man was so quick, so agile in the removal of the lug nuts and the rise of the jack.

"William. Come on."

He finally turned and followed Maggie to room 19.

Her mother wasn't there, either.

"She knew we'd be here about now," Maggie said. "Her not being here is no accident. She knows we can't walk around fucking Juarez, the most dangerous city in the goddamn world, hoping to bump into her. Let's just wait up near her room. She'll come back when she's ready."

William and Maggie sat on a little bench just outside the motel room. William rested his head against the tan stucco wall. Maggie was sitting Indian style.

"Do you know that I always wanted to be a painter? I have this idea of chronicling the emaciation of woman. From fat cherubs to skeletons. From dark skinned Mestizos to blue eyed girls from Indiana." Maggie blew a bubble with her gum. "Problem is I can't paint worth shit."

William kicked at a pebble. William did know. He knew she wanted to be a little bit of everything.

From down below, a taxi pulled onto the gravel next to the van.

"She's here," Maggie said.

William could just make out the shape of the woman exiting the cab. She was medium built, medium height. Her long black hair, with silver strands that gave her a halo of light, was in two braids that hung halfway down her back. Her clothing was simple. A white knit shirt and jeans. The woman was getting something out of the taxi's trunk. The green door closed and William could see her face. It was Maggie but older. Round cheeks, big almond eyes, small mouth that protruded just a little, maybe a slight overbite. He couldn't see the freckles on her nose but he knew they were there. He couldn't see the wrinkle along the brow, just one, nearer the hairline than the eyebrow but he knew it was there, too. Maybe she had a few more, on places Maggie didn't just yet. William would have to wait and see. The woman closed the trunk and paid the cab driver. William saw her look up and spot Maggie and him. She shook her head and walked briskly to the stairwell.

William and Maggie stood. Maggie's mother labored up each step. Realizing he was being rude, William moved towards the landing and motioned for her to hand him her bags.

She looked at him with intense focus. "Who are you? And what are you doing with my daughter? And what do you want with my bag?" She pointed her finger at him, and William backed up against the railing.

"Mama, this is the man Tío told you about," Maggie said, stepping in. There wasn't even the attempt of an embrace.

"What man?"

"William. This is William. He's my neighbor and he's giving you, us, his van. So that you can transport your produce."

Mrs. Cruces now gave Maggie the once over, a gift of hers that seemed preternatural and infinite.

"Are you pregnant?" She wagged her finger at the two of them.

"Mama!"

William nearly fell over. His face flushed so hard that it had turned white.

"It needed to be asked," Mrs. Cruces said with childlike candor. "Now, let's go to my room and get out of the heat and ready for a good night's rest." She placed the handle of her bag in William's clenched fist.

"Where were you, Mama? The guy up front said you had already checked in."

"Having dinner with a friend. Now, let's get some sleep. We have quite a road trip ahead of us in the morning."

William was told to sleep in the bathtub. Anna, Maggie's mother, lined the bottom of the tub with the comforter from the bed. She and Maggie used the bathroom while William stood outside the door. When the women were finished, Anna gave William a pillow from her bed, wished him a goodnight and then closed the bathroom door. William stood there in the dark for a moment, then he began undressing. He climbed into the tub and stared blankly at the water-stained ceiling, made visible by a light shining through the small window above the shower.

William tried to summarize all of his failures but he had none. He'd never failed and never succeeded. He'd just been.

He thought of all the ways he might want to die. In his sleep would be best but he knew he was too young for that. He didn't have pills. He didn't have a gun. Hanging was too macabre and fraught with the very real possibility of failing. Nothing worse than a failed suicide, he thought. He would just have to find a high place, a very high place, and take just one step forward. Maybe two.

Maggie hung up some clothes in the closet.

"I need to do laundry," she said.

Anna had changed into her nightgown. It was long, with lavender ruffles along the cuffs, the hem and the collar. She fluffed her pillow.

"I know we won't have time. I just hope I don't stink up the van," Maggie said, laughing.

"Quit trying so hard."

"What?" Maggie said.

"It's been fifteen years since I've seen you. You think I care about laundry?" Anna stood near the edge of the bed. She was brushing her long hair, over and over, looking in the mirror that hung over the desk. She made no attempt to look at her daughter.

"No, I suppose you don't. I was just making small talk." Maggie felt her chest tighten.

"You look very pretty, Margarita. Except for that tattoo. *Cuchina*."

"I was drunk when I got that," Maggie said, dropping her hands down to her ankle to hide the skull with the knife through the right eye socket, as she sat on the bed.

"Is that supposed to make me feel better about it?" Anna asked. Maggie could hear in her voice the same thing she had heard for those first fifteen years. She had learned to ignore it, like the classic man and wife taking out the garbage duet, but now she heard it – disappointment, disapproval – again for the first time. Her mother's voice was high pitched but not piercing. She saved that for the subtext. It took Maggie's breath away.

William heard the conversation from inside the bathroom. Such sadness, he thought. The distance between the women was ocean sized.

Firecrackers went off somewhere outside and William wondered what the sparkle looked like.

"Night, Mama," Maggie said as she slid into the twin bed with the thin sheets. She could hear her mother's breathing and knew she was already asleep. Maggie heard the gunshots go off and flinched instinctively. Then she wrapped herself up as best she could and waited for sleep to overtake her.

23

Anna flung open the dilapidated drapes and the sun ricocheted off the dresser mirror into Maggie's closed eyes. She rolled over to avoid the glare.

"It's 6:00 already, *meija*. *Levantate*." Her mother's voice was different in the morning. It was clear and succinct, easier to listen to.

Maggie put a pillow over her head.

"Long day ahead of us. Best to get an early start."

Maggie thought of the long day to be spent three feet away from her mother and tried not to shudder. Yes, she thought, best to get an early start. That was the only way to achieve an early end.

"Okay, I'm up," she said, flinging the bedding off. "Where's William?"

"I heard him stirring earlier."

William had been up since five. The cold ceramic tile was unforgiving and now a crick in his neck overtook the pain in his face. He stared at the tile that crawled up the shower wall. It was green, blue and yellow, with mold built up in the grout. He turned over on his side and began to count the tiles. If he could count to ten thousand, he wouldn't do it, he wouldn't kill himself. He'd be saved.

At seventy-seven, a blue tile, chipped on its bottom left corner, he heard something from the other room. It was Anna. While Maggie would have gotten out of bed with a thud, both feet hitting the ground at the same time, Anna was different. She put one foot down, then the other. A shot of light suddenly burst through the bottom of the bathroom door and he remembered where he was in his counting, seventy-seven blue. William got out of the tub. He put his ear to the bathroom door. He listened to her and this made him happy, if only for a moment. William strained to detect the sounds of Anna's feet shuffling toward the closet and a faint rustling as she took off her nightgown. He heard her folding it and wondered what she looked like without it. Then she dressed. He thought he could hear her pants rub up her leg and then the zipper being zipped, then her blouse being buttoned. He wondered if her eyes were watching her fingers or instead watching Maggie, to see if she was still asleep or faking sleep. Then Anna was on the move again. He heard a chair get pulled out. Makeup application and hair brushing, likely at the small mirror above the dresser. And then the sound of the chair being pushed back in. She was near the door now, near the dresser. William thought maybe he could hear her breathe. She was that close. He held his breath. This gave him a thrill, though he didn't know why. Drawers were opened as she packed her things into her small tote bag. She used her phone at some point. Though she whispered into the cell phone, William caught most of what she said. Maggie was fine. The older man was pleasant and quiet. She hadn't been able to save Sotera. Another one gone, this one to Texas. *Que lastíma*, she said repeatedly.

Eavesdropping was like a drug to William, a sedative. He didn't want to admit how much he loved it. He knew she probably had to use the bathroom but didn't want the moment to end, so he made sure she couldn't hear that he was awake. He softly put his back against the cold door until she hung up the phone. Then it was over. William seized with some unknown fear and crawled back into his bathtub bed.

Seventy-eight, he thought as the mold spread from a blue tile to a yellow.

"Coming in, William. Hope you're decent." Maggie knocked, waited for a few moments and then opened the door. He was sitting on the edge of the sink, staring out of the small window. Maggie closed the door behind her.

"Why the hell do you look so sad?"

Because I'm dying, he thought. Because I'm already dead. He wanted to find some puerile humor in his turn to the macabre, comedy in the blackness. But he could not.

Maggie looked outside.

"Looks like a nice day," she said, then she stopped and grabbed William's shoulders. She eyed him intently.

"Listen," she said in a pointed whisper, "I need your help today. I just need to get through this trip. I need you to have my back. If Anna and I start going at it, do something to break us up. It's been fifteen years since I've seen her. I'm tripped out right now. Like I'm fifteen all over again, but I'm not. I'm old. I'm confused. It's not a good place to be."

William handed Maggie her toothbrush. He lifted his eyebrow then he walked out of the bathroom, his arms hanging off his shoulders like wet straw.

Anna waited by the front door as William and Maggie finished packing.

"She's all but tapping her goddamn feet at us," Maggie said in William's ear.

"Almost ready, Mama," she said over her shoulder. Anna didn't move, let alone respond.

Maggie zipped up her bag. William did the same. They met Anna at the door.

"Okay, all set. Let's go."

They reached the van and William loaded the suitcases in the back. His neck still hurt but he didn't let the women know.

24

"So, Mama, I say we just hightail it home. No stopping. What d'ya say?" The wind was whipping in from outside, swirling Anna's hair in silver spools like a ghostly whirlpool. She sat with perfect posture in the backseat, wearing khaki capris. She had on a basic white t-shirt. Her hands were folded school-girl style in her lap. She sat in the only seat still left in the back of the van, his father having removed all other seats to make more room for his floral arrangements. Next to her were luggage, some food wrappers and empty soda cans. William had a quiet urge to clean it all up.

"Well, that is a very good plan," Anna said.

"I thought so, too. Let's just get the hell home," Maggie said.

William noticed that Maggie's accent had changed from the mestizo English of Los Angeles, where words often bled into some third language, to a more refined Spanish. She took the time to roll her Rs and enunciate her *tildes* cleanly.

"Yes, get the hell home." Anna aped as she twisted the pendant of the Virgin Mary that hung from a thin gold chain around her neck. It made

William think about Pedro and he checked his pocket to make sure the wooden rabbit's foot was still there. It was.

"Or we could make a day of it here," Anna said. "I know there's a nice street fair going on in southern Juarez. We could stop there and show William a little bit of Mexican culture."

"Mama? A street fair in Juarez? Are you joking?"

"I will not be held captive by terrorists. Not in my own country."

"We read about people being killed. It seems to make the news all the time. Every day. And it's usually right here. Why tempt fate?"

"I can say the same thing about where you live. Every day. And please let's not talk about tempting fate."

"What?"

"A fifteen year old leaves her home and her family to move a world away."

"But I made it."

"Says who?"

"I say. I made it."

"And so will we. It's a picnic, it's a party, not a drug deal."

"But we should get home," Maggie said in defeat.

"I've decided. We are going. It will be fun. William, don't you think we could all use a little fun?"

William nodded.

William felt a wave of nerves as Anna sat behind him in the van. He reached back and retrieved his bag. He felt Anna's eyes on him as he rummaged near and around her. He found his journal and then wrote in it for the first time since he'd left Los Angeles. His words slashed across the page as the van rumbled over the rough pavement:

She drops the angle of her jaw when she speaks to her daughter. This says something but I don't know what.

She tends to quickly bite her bottom lip with her two front teeth just before she speaks. Maggie does this too, but she hasn't the overbite her mother has. It looks different when Anna does it. It looks more dangerous.

She defends herself too quickly. No one is judging her. Maggie is not. Maggie just wants to go home. Though I wonder where she means by home. Wherever home is, it means more to Anna, even if Maggie has a greater need to get there.

I can see this world that passes by me in short scenes from movies. I try and find places for the dialogue, but I get it wrong every time.

She came here to save someone. To Juarez. To save a cousin or maybe a niece from the United States. I am the evil to the North, all the long silent day. I am nothing good and she knows this. She sees me as American. White and male. Maggie is right to fear her. She knows that I am nothing but rotten. A quiet rotted man who is haunted. I see her staring at me, her gaze penetrating right through my skin. I just want to keep writing but I have nothing more to write about.

"What are you writing, William?" Anna asked.

William shook his head. *Nothing*. He put the book down and forced a smile.

"It's just what he does when he's bored, Mama," added Maggie.

25

The street fair was on the outskirts of town in a park lined with large poplar trees on one side and a small street on the other. A patch of dead grass served as a parking lot. Throngs of people lined the street, which had scores of booths, carnival games, a small farmer's market selling fried squash and salted pistachios. Even more people filled the park. The air smelled of sweet bread and *carne asada*.Children begged for churros and cotton candy. Men lined up for *cerveza* and pork rinds. A large cloud formation made an explosion of white in the sky, which was otherwise pristine and blue.

"Let's have some lunch," Anna said. "William, what do you think of tamales?"

William nodded. He wasn't hungry but feigned enthusiasm.

"Good."

It was strange to William that Anna never asked about his silence. Had Maggie pulled her aside and told her? Maybe she knew all along. Or perhaps she never even realized that William had been silent their entire time together.

A dog trotted by William and stopped to smell his crotch. William blushed.

"He likes you. We should feed him something," Anna said, bending down to pet the mutt.

Animals soften her, William thought. He liked that.

They stood under the shade of a poplar and ate tamales from tin foil wraps and watched the fiesta as they ate. Maggie bought *horchata* for herself and Anna, and a beer for William.

"You should stay away from bangs, Margarita," Anna said between bites. "It keeps your face from looking round."

Maggie didn't respond. Some kids were kicking around a soccer ball.

"I'm gonna go and run around, find my inner child," Maggie said. She took a final sip of her drink and then ran towards the kids. The older boys circled around her and demonstrated to her the proper way to kick the ball.

"She could always break hearts," Anna said as she watched Maggie laugh with the boys. "She did it even as a child. Little boys would surround her at church or at the market. They were always fascinated by her."

The two of them sat on a blanket and watched in quiet as the day unfolded. The sun moved to the center of the sky. William wanted another beer but sat on his hands. Anna kept looking at him. She stared right at him and then looked away, toward the ground or at some kid crying for more candy.

William kept his eye on Maggie and her gang of soccer boys but could feel Anna's stare. He was used to being invisible. The attention made him nervous. He really wanted another beer.

"Let's go for a walk," Anna said.

William nodded.

They walked along the outskirts of the grounds. William found a couple of red dahlias and matched them with white frangipani. He put the three flowers together and plucked off the petals. Anna watched him do this and smiled.

"How did you learn to understand Spanish? Did your parents speak Spanish?"

William nodded. He had to lie. How could he tell her that he no idea how he learned it? He just understood it the same way he understood English. He had heard that blind people often have their other senses heightened. Perhaps a similar phenomenon had occurred with him. He hadn't ever given it much thought. The words drifted into his ears and they formed sentences. That was all.

"We're safe here. We are too far south for all the danger. This is the nice part of Juarez, because it isn't really Juarez. I thought you should know. I did this to make her squirm a bit," Anna said with a half-smile.

A burro ambled by them with three laughing kids atop its back.

"I feel like that burro every day," Anna said. Then she laughed and went to grab the beer bottle in William's hand but it was empty. "You need another beer, Mr. William." She said this in English and William thought of the women he'd heard speaking in whispers on buses, the women who cleaned the homes of the wealthy, north of Sunset Boulevard.

The burro stopped a few feet away from the two of them and snorted. It dug for stalks of grass in the dirt. The kids were kicking it in the haunches and yelling at it to move.

"*Vamos, vamos*," they shouted but the burro stayed put.

"That burro isn't going anywhere," Anna said as she got up. "I'll go get a few more beers. Meet you back at our spot. Maggie bringing me that *horchata* was kind of silly." Anna walked away but kept looking back

The wind kicked up and William watched it play with the tendrils of Anna's silver hair. He walked back towards their blanket, picking a few more flowers as he did. He wanted to beautify their spot as much as he could.

She came back with three beers and *flautas*.

William stood up to take the food from her.

"You're eating this with chilies that I grow on my farm. Not the exact same ones, of course, but the same kind. Most gringos can't handle this, but I think you can."

William took the plate of food and bit into the fried dish. The flavor of the chili started out sweet but then it turned.

"Here, drink," she said. "I guess we'll have to work you up to that."

William feigned a heart attack and fell to the ground.

"You're worse than the burro. Get up."

William got up.

"Do you mind me asking what happened to your face?"

William balled his hands into fists, punched himself in the face and fell back down to the ground.

"Did you even get one punch in?"

William stayed motionless on the ground.

"I'll take that as a no," Anna said, laughing.

He got back up and dusted off the dirt.

"I hate violence. I'm glad you didn't fight back. It shows mettle and character."

Anna saw the dahlias on the blanket.

"Are those for me?"

William nodded and sipped his beer.

"This is our flower. It's the Mexican national flower." She brought the flowers to her nose. Then she held out the flowers in front of her. "Funny, I always thought this flower looked like a pinwheel of blades." Then she set down the makeshift bouquet.

William opened a beer for Anna and handed it to her. They both sat down, legs curled beneath them.

Later, Maggie came back, sweaty and out of breath.

"Beer? Who brought beer?"

After nightfall, the streets cleared out. A few kids played with sparklers. Some drunk men were singing along to a man strumming a guitar. The words were lost in the drunken warble but it was a happy song that promised love would work out for the faithful and the brave. The evening was cool but not cold and William imagined this was what the Fourth of July must feel like for most Americans. The gentle buzz of family and friends, the just-out-of-reach feeling that one is a witness to the formation of nostalgia. The distinct smells and sounds of fiesta, of laughing, of reverie. It was nice, he admitted to himself, but just for one furtive moment. But then the niceness of the moment was gone.

The three of them walked to the van.

"Mama, that was really fun. Great idea."

"Did you get any of those boys' numbers?"

"Mama!" Maggie playfully slapped at her shoulder.

William walked a few steps behind. What's wrong with me, he thought.

Anna and Maggie were walking arm in arm towards the van, whispering things to one another.

I'm depressed, he admitted to himself. Even as he looked at Anna, even as she snuck a peek back at him, I'm depressed, he thought. It's finally happened.

26

When he was a young child, William hated when he would hear his mother making her way down the hallway late at night. He could hear her coming and it would wake him up immediately. Never his brother, who notoriously slept through earthquakes, rioting, nightmares. But always William. His eyes would pop open by the second or third shuffle. She's too tired to even pick up her feet, William would think. He pictured her white slippers rowing above the green shag carpet like a canoe on Lake Hattawhatta, where he'd gone to summer camp for one day. (They sent him home by six in the evening for lack of camp spirit when he refused to chant the camp motto). As she neared his room, her shuffling would get louder and louder. As William heard her nearing his door, his breathing would increase. Then, as she reached his door, the shuffling would stop. Everything stopped. Moments would pass like those freeze-framed final minutes of arithmetic class on a perfect Friday afternoon. Sometimes, on the good nights, she would turn around and row back down the green canal towards the kitchen or her room, wherever adults went deep in the night. But most times, she would slowly open the door, its creaks and moans always so real to William, as if the door wasn't just an opening to his room but a person with thoughts and wounds and important things to say, and let herself in.

"Billy?" She would ask. "Billy, I know you're up. Can Mama slip in bed with you?"

William would nod, though she couldn't see this, his brown cow eyes wide and alert.

"Scoot it over, Billy." She slid next to him on the bed and put her arms under her head and looked at the ceiling, like his brother did when he talked about girls during backyard camping nights. William felt trapped between his mother's thin body and the coldness of the wall.

"I just don't know what to do, Billy. I just don't know what to do. It's too much. It's just too much." William forever wondered why his mother repeated most things she'd said, as if saying them twice made them twice as profound.

William would pray to god for his brother to wake up, for his father to come running down the hall and save him and save her.

"Give me a kiss on the cheek, Billy. Maybe for the last time. Maybe for the last time." And little Billy would kiss her on the cheek for what he was sure would be the last time. His mother would then get up and shuffle back down the hallway to somewhere else and William would wake up the next morning afraid to move, afraid that she was no longer there and afraid of what he might find in her place.

27

Anna and Maggie reached the van. From behind, they looked like salt-and-pepper twins. We become them, William thought, we become them in spite of ourselves.

"Everyone in the Flower Van," Maggie laughed. "The Big Blue *Vehico de Flores de William de Los Angeles de California de Mexico.*"

They were silent for a long time as they traveled south. Anna sat in a refined pose and looked straight ahead, occasionally allowing her eyes to study William but just for a second. She was more concerned with the horizon.

Maggie fiddled with the radio but it was mostly static. She strummed her fingers along the steering wheel but stopped whenever her mother gave a warning cough. William didn't do anything. His mind was numb and vacuous and he felt like a dandelion, ready to be blown into innocuous bits of fluff.

"Damn. I need to stop and use a bathroom," Maggie said.

"It can't wait until we need gas?"

"No. I need water, too. There's an exit coming up. William, you need anything?"

William shook his head. He thumbed Pedro's wooden rabbit's foot over and over though the pocket of his jeans.

Maggie pulled the van up to the small store. She kept the van running.

"I'll be back in three."

The van idled with a heavy rumble. The exhaust pipe poured out plumes of black smoke, a coughing mess.

"This vehicle is in good shape?"

William nodded but only half-heartedly. He didn't really know.

From his vantage point, he could see just where the cash register was. But there was no clerk there. He looked at the cars that lined the makeshift dirt parking lot. He counted ten. Maybe eleven. But no one was outside smoking or loitering near the archaic telephone. He could see no movement in the store at all, which was just a little five and dime, as his mother might've said. Why wouldn't there be a clerk at the counter?

He unbuckled his seat belt. Something was wrong.

"William, do you need something? I can go in for you." William stepped out and closed the door on Anna's offer. She quickly reopened it.

"What's wrong? Stay inside, William."

William put his hand out to stop her, like his mere hand were enough to drop anchor on the obdurate force with the silver strands and pleasant round face.

She slapped his hand down.

He caught it and squeezed. With his other hand, he pointed to the backseat with firm direction.

"You're white as a sheet." Anna looked inside. She caught on. "Where is everyone? Where's Maggie?"

She broke free from William's grip and ran to the front of the store, which was still painted green and red to mark September's Independence Day. William was right behind her. He was calm. Shockingly calm. The decorated window ended three feet above the ground and they both hunched down so that the wall covered their bodies. Then, very slowly, they peered inside, like first-time thieves.

"She's right there," Anna whispered. Maggie was inside. She had the water in her hand. She was gesticulating something very dramatic. As if her hands could explain more than her words. William scooted down to try and get a glimpse of the person she was speaking with.

He strained his neck and just when he couldn't strain any longer, he saw the man. He was a large man with a heavy beard and a shock of black hair, coarse, like raven's feathers. He was nodding at Maggie. Behind him, were about fifteen other people, all men. They looked bored. It seemed so unfair, all those men against little Maggie.

Not again, he thought. Not again, he thought, just like his mother would've said with words.

"What do you see?"

He put up his finger to silence her. She listened. Then he motioned her not to move, not one inch. She nodded. He closed his eyes and then, in the quickest movement possible, rose to his feet and barged into the front of the store.

He put his hands up, for no other reason than that's what he had seen people in similar situations do in the movies and on television.

"*Maricon*."The big bearded man said. "Who the fuck is this piece of shit?" A few of the men laughed.

"He's my uncle," Maggie lied."He's very rich. He's white. Please just let us go and we'll be quiet."

William glanced back at the window. He couldn't see Anna, which meant neither could the men.

"Shut up, you stupid cunt," The man said in English, as William looked back towards the posse. While he couldn't see the gun from his crouched spot under the window, he assumed one was there and now here it was, in the man's left hand, being waved effortlessly like a small flag.

William scanned the room quickly. Behind the mass of men he could see packages of some sort, hundreds of them, wrapped in brown paper, all the same size, stacked up as if about to be moved or shipped.

He and Maggie made eye contact. She smiled at him, one of those smiles that was resigned with the fate of no escape, no hope.

"What the fuck are you two doing here? Do you know nothing? How stupid are you two fuckers?" The man with the gun laughed at his line of questioning.

"We didn't know anything. I just needed water. Now please, can we please just go?"

"Now, princess, we couldn't do that. Not now that we know we are in the presence of a white man."

"And a rich white man at that," one of the chorus members added.

"A rich white man can fetch just as much as the rich white stuff," added another.

"Kill the stupid bitch and let's bring the gringo to Hector," the big bearded man said casually.

"I'm not cleaning up if you do it inside," said one of the men standing in the back.

"Shut up, *puta*," said the big bearded man. He then twirled his gun like John Wayne might have on set and stuck it in an invisible holster, which was really his belt. "Bang, bang," he said, and disappeared into a back room.

One of the men, a small man with pock-marked skin and John 3:16 tattooed on his left cheek, stepped forward. He reached behind his back and pulled out a small pistol. He had the look of someone desperate to make his name known. He walked towards Maggie.

William tried to rush in front of him but three of the men grabbed him and frog marched him away. William struggled. A punch landed in his gut and William doubled over in pain. The pain in his stomach somehow showed in the wince on his face.

The pock-marked man aimed the gun right at Maggie, the end of the barrel touching her forehead.

"Fucking bitch. We warned you fucking reporters to stay the hell out of our business."

"Why would you think I was a reporter? I'm not a reporter," she said.

"Then this won't be news."

The front door opened for a third time.

Anna walked in. She was calm. She took long strides. She reached the pock- marked man and spoke directly to him.

"You guys are doing this all wrong. You are asking for trouble. You want to make money selling drugs to Americans? Fine. But don't kill them in cold blood. Don't awaken the sleeping giant."

The pock-marked man looked at her, then to his friends, then back to her.

The big bearded man had come back from wherever he had gone to.

"You mean the government?" He laughed. "They don't give a shit, lady."

"I mean public opinion. You think killing this girl, this pretty American girl, is going to go over well with the pollsters? With the white-bread churchgoers of Texas nobility? This is the wrong thing to do. You let the Americans live. You let them live so they can buy your product."

"And who the fuck are you anyway?" The pock-marked man yapped.

"I'm trying to help you make more money." Anna walked to Maggie and redirected the gun towards her own face. "If you're going to shoot anyone, if you have some desire for blood, kill me. Spare the Americans, kill the old Mexican lady. There are at least three times a day when I would probably thank you for it."

"This is fucking ridiculous," the bearded man said as he pushed the pock-marked man aside. "You don't tell us how we run things. You don't get to say a word."

"Kill them all," the pock-marked man said.

"Shut the hell up, Juan."

The pock-marked man, Juan, shot the big bearded man a look.

The bearded man crossed the room to where William was being held.

"You. How much can you give us so that these two *putas* can live?" William tried to reach for his wallet but the men wouldn't let him go.

"Check him for a gun."

The men frisked him.

"How much?"

The bearded man waited. Then he grabbed William' face with his hand. He squeezed hard and William winced.

"I will not ask again. How. Fucking. Much. Or the ladies die."

The pock-marked man pulled the trigger back on cue and aimed it at Maggie. His hand was shaking. His lips formed a fake crescent moon of a smile and he wiped his brow with his free hand.

"It's no use asking him," Anna whispered. "He can't speak."

"What?" The bearded man asked.

"He's a mute. He can't speak. You'd have a better chance getting those tomatoes to recite Octavio Paz." She pointed to the tomatoes on sale.

"The bitch is lying," Juan said. "The bitch is a fucking *mentirosa*."

"I told you to be quiet, Juan."The bearded man said through clenched teeth.

"Don't you fucking tell me to be quiet, you *puta maricon*."

The bearded man turned and looked over his shoulder at Juan.

"Shut up."

"Don't you fucking tell me to shut up, *puta maricon*."

"Juan, shut the fuck up."

"You shut up, you fucking *maricon*."

The bearded man turned and looked at Juan. Juan opened his mouth and flicked his tongue. The bearded man pointed his gun at Juan. And then he shot him.

The pock-marked man, tattooed with a Bible verse, crumbled to the ground.

"Fucking pest, always barking. Worse than a fucking street dog," the bearded man said.

William looked at Anna, whose face remained stoic. Maggie had let out a small cry. None of the other men moved.

A door opened from the back. A tall, thin man walked through. Power emanated from him despite his slight build. But the power seemed to be escaping him by the second, a deflating dominance with just the smallest of leaks. He didn't look at any of them, including Juan or Maggie or Anna.

"General, we've got this under control," said the big bearded man. The General stepped over the pock-marked man moaning and squirming on the floor.

"I can tell," the General said.

He walked briskly towards William and looked him square in the eyes.

"You can't speak?"

William shook his head.

"But you understand Spanish?"

He nodded.

"Can you understand sign language?"

And to Maggie's surprise, William once again nodded.

"You three are coming with me."

28

Maggie was trembling as the she rode in the backseat with Anna and William. The General had tied them up with hemp rope and Maggie was glad she was in the middle. It made her feel safe. Or if not exactly safe then at least safer. Anna watched the General. Every time he looked at them in the rearview mirror she glared right back at him.

I did this, William thought. I wished for suicide and now we are going to be killed. He wished that he had opened that door and rolled out onto the asphalt, until he found the desert floor, where he could lie in a quiet heap with the sage and cacti and the coils of dead skin shed by a sidewinder.

"I'm sorry to have to tie you up," the man said without looking back. "It's just a precaution." His voice was different in the car. It was deflated, almost flat. Certainly distracted by something other than Anna, William and Maggie.

"We don't have any weapons."

"You have hands and fingers. And mouths."

"Can you at least tell us where we're going?"

"You'll find out soon enough. I just need to borrow the silent idiot there. Then I will take you back and let you go. I promise."

"To your gang of henchmen?"

The General laughed at this.

"More like fourth-tier pirates," he said under his breath.

Anna scoffed. "They seemed more than ready to kill us, like they do each other."

Maggie hit her and glared.

Without slowing down his truck, the General turned his head around and put his finger on his mouth. Be quiet, he said without saying.

Anna closed her eyes for a long blink.

The man's phone rang. He turned back around and answered it.

"Yes." The General nodded as he spoke.

"Yes."

"All day every day." He said this with a sadness that deflated him even further. His cheeks sucked in air as best they could and he appeared gaunt and sick.

"If only I could."

"Right now? It's taking me everything not to do it. Every ounce of my strength."

"I can't do that right now." The General looked back at his cargo. "I'm, uh, on a very important errand."

"Okay, okay. I'll do it." The General was being strong-armed. Maggie and Anna looked at each quizzically.

"See you soon."

He hung up his phone.

"We have to make a brief stop. It won't take long but I have no choice. I have to go."

"We really are in a great hurry, sir," Anna said.

The General slammed on the brakes and the car came skidding to a stop.

He turned his whole body around and aimed his gun at Maggie.

He pulled back the trigger.

Anna held her breath. Maggie closed her eyes.

"Will you please help me not shoot her by shutting the fuck up?" The General was sweating. Large beads of sweat on his brow, at his temples, through his armpits.

Anna nodded.

"Thank you."

William looked at Maggie and wondered how long the scar from the end of the barrel of the gun would remain on her forehead.

Twenty minutes later, they pulled into the dirt parking lot of a small church. The wooden cross that perched atop the steeple was bent slightly, as if a bunch of atheist crows had played a small joke.

We're going to die, Maggie kept thinking, over and over. This is the part where the evil man turns and shoots us, when he realized we have nothing of value to keep us as hostages. Fifteen years ago was the last time she was sure she was going to die. Oh, how nice it would be find a god and make him promise to make things work in the next world.

"I have to run in here for a little while," the man said from the front seat.

"Is it safe to keep us here in the heat?" Anna asked.

"It won't be long."

"I'm not dying in the parking lot of a church. This is ridiculous. All we wanted was a little water. And now we find ourselves in the middle of nowhere doing who knows what."

"No one's dying." The General was icy but resolved. The General rubbed his cheek, which now had dark stubble with hints of gray here and there. He looked at the church then back at Anna.

"Fine. But I have a gun. And I know everyone in this town. There is nowhere to run and hide. And don't speak a word about anything you've seen. People might believe you but no one will do a fucking thing to help you. No one plays the hero."

William wondered if that was from some American movie. It sounded like it was but he couldn't place it. The man reached back and quickly undid the knots that bound the three. Then he got out of the car and unlocked one of the doors.

Maggie wondered what the bullet would feel like. Cold and then warm, together at first, cold and warm then split, the rush of warm first, like a punctured fever and then the cold, setting in like winter ice until everything, every lake and road, was frozen over and solid.

Anna, then Maggie and finally William stumbled out. The man grabbed William by the arm and directed the girls to start walking.

29

There was a small party inside the church. Fifteen or twenty people, mostly men, spoke in gentle murmurs and sipped coffee that was brewing in a large silver pot on a fold-out table. William looked around for a priest, hoping maybe a man of the cloth would sense the incongruent nature of their little tribe but none was present. The General kept his hand firmly grasped around William's upper arm. He whispered to William that the gun was still in the pocket of his jacket.

"Hector," said a man from behind. This man seemed to be the only person at the party who knew the General. "You made it. And you brought friends, I see." He smiled warmly at Anna and Maggie. He gave Hector a quick hug. "Hector, let the man go. If he makes a run for it, well, he won't find anything nearby to appease him." The man laughed at his own joke. Anna and William looked at each other. "I don't know if you're quite ready to be a sponsor but I applaud your trying to help."

"Yes, well, you have been so good to me, I figured it's my turn to help someone else. He's in really bad shape. That was my errand. I was talking him off the ledge."

"And the ladies?"

"Just friends," Anna said and smiled charmingly.

"No fucking way," Maggie said, which induced a sharp, pointed glance by the General.

Maggie had done her time in AA. A DUI on a night after just one too many margaritas with Lupe had scared her sober for a long time. She did the thirty meetings in thirty days. She listened to the sad stories, the crashes, both vehicular and spiritual, the bottoms, the man who kept showing up to the meeting drunk and then crying for help. The lady who blew a .4 and crashed her Bentley into the front of the crack house by the Coliseum. Maggie remembered the lady who fell off the wagon after five years of sobriety and died of alcohol poisoning a day later, her body not used to the quantity her mind craved. She recalled the lonely diatribes, the broken childhoods, the bad dads and cold moms that led to Tuesday nights at 7:00 in that coffee shop off Pico. She lasted a year. But in the end, the Serenity Prayer never brought her the serenity it promised. In the end, she felt all this talk of recovery was its own addiction. In the end, she missed having a drink but learned to do so without driving. Usually.

She never, ever thought she would be in the middle of Mexico at an AA meeting with a drug dealer, her mother and a mute white man.

"Please sit, everyone. Thank you all for coming. My name is Thomas and I'm an alcoholic." Thomas reminded Maggie of many of the regulars at her bar back at home. He was short, plain, riddled with wrinkles and deep brown eyes that had trouble looking straight ahead for too long.

The meeting went on and on. People shared their stories. William felt exhausted by all of it. And yet he was mesmerized. He kept thinking we are all the same. We are all the same. We all become what we're supposed to become. He didn't know why he was thinking these things, he didn't know what any of it meant.

Hector never let go of his arm and it was starting to pulse with pain but he wasn't angry. There was nothing to get angry about. This man with a gun at his side, who had killed and robbed and who knows what else, was just like him.

The wooden pews were oddly unforgiving. He kept looking over at Anna. And she would look back and smile at him and he felt happy for a moment.

"We have time for one more testimonial," Thomas said. Hector's sponsor urged Hector forward but he didn't budge.

"Hector, it's time for you to finally speak," the man whispered. But Hector just shook his head and dug his fingers into William's arm.

Finally, after a moment where nothing happened, a small round man, maybe forty, stood up a few rows behind William and the women. He grunted loudly as he did so. He shuffled slowly down his row, bumping others as he made his way, those sitting down like during a bathroom break in the middle of a movie. He coughed three times as he shuffled – loud, deliberate coughs meant to be heard. Once he reached the aisle, his walk was just as deliberate, just as loud as his coughs. He dug his feet into the red carpet, then lifted them heavily, one after the other, as if some invisible devil was nailing him to the floor with each step. Beads of sweat glistened on his face in the hot, sticky church.

He reached the podium. He looked out at his fellow alcoholics and William felt another odd twinge of camaraderie with a stranger.

"As I stand here today talking to you, I am very grateful. For that, I should fall down on the floor and weep and thank god."

His voice was blue collar, sounding as though it had spent time in the mines, never finding the yellow bird.

"I have been sober for seventeen years because of that very truth – that I *can* stand here and talk with you. You all have been my saving grace for these seventeen years of sobriety. We have seen so much, haven't we?"

He stopped to remember some of those things but didn't share.

"Because, let me tell you, each and every day in each and every year, through everything seen or unseen, I have wanted to drink. I have wanted nothing more than to walk down to the bar at the end of my street and order a tequila and beer and then order ten more of each. But I haven't because I can stand here and talk with you people."

Another pause. William thought this man should be on stage. He was ugly and fat with poor elocution but he owned his space with the presence of a movie star. The woman next to him quit chewing her gum, her mouth open and the gum resting precariously in between her front teeth and tongue, nearly paralyzed as she hung on his next word. Another man, sitting one row up and a seat over, looked as though he was going to cry. And he also looked like a man who never cried.

"My wife left me today."

The woman chewed her gum once before it froze again between teeth and tongue. The man who might be his friend, put his head down. Everyone else stared ahead, with great intent. A few people gasped.

His voice hardened now, transitioning from blue collar to crushed gravel.

"She left me after four years of marriage. She told me she wanted something more. What? I asked her. What more could you want? I make a good living. I provide for her and her two children. I don't beat her. I make her life easy. We make love. I cook from time to time. I do everything a man is supposed to do when he respects and loves his wife. And I don't drink! How many wives can say that about their husbands? Not many, I guess. She could not answer me when I asked what *more* she wanted. She stood there, a smug smile, her bags packed. I want to get angry right now and I can feel the anger rising up in me like a big wave. I can feel it rising up in me and I can feel it needing to escape so that it can blow up everything around me. So that it can... I love my wife very much. I wanted to spend eternity protecting her, loving her. I wanted to shield her from the shit and pain that I had known in my life prior to meeting her. You've heard my stories. I won't tell them again. But I can't shield her from anything. I can't protect her from the *more* that she craves. More, more, more. We all know something about that in here don't we? The endless desire for more. Well fuck it. I can't tell her that trying to get *more* is a fool's game. She'll have to figure it out all by herself. So fuck her and fuck me. I won't tell her the secrets I've learned, I won't protect her with my knowledge. Only the dirt can. Only the goddamn dirt can protect us and keep our secrets."

Then the man pulled a silver flask from his pocket. No one in the crowd flinched.

"To seventeen years."

The man drank the contents of the flask in one long gulp. Then he walked down the center aisle of the room and left through the main doors, slamming them shut as he walked out.

Anna jumped at the sound.

William put his head down.

"That was fucking awesome," Maggie said to no one in particular.

30

Thomas walked quickly up to the front of the church and tried to regain control of the meeting. The murmur of the crowd pulsed like a cocaine heartbeat. He had everyone stand up and hold hands. The Serenity Prayer came and went.

"He wasn't working the steps," Hector's sponsor said in a reproachful tone a few moments after the meeting was over. "See, Hector? Let this be a lesson. Even after seventeen years, if you don't work the steps, you can relapse. You can't let the circumstances of your life determine whether or not you drink."

Hector looked at his three captives.

"I know."

"And you, how did you feel about it?" The sponsor asked William. William smiled and gave the man a thumbs up.

"What does that mean?"

"He's a man of few words," Hector said for William. "Listen, I have to go. Get these three home. Thank you for making me attend today. I'll call you before I go to bed."

"That's right, you will." The sponsor and Hector hugged awkwardly. "Very nice to meet you, ladies. Sir." Then he left to go and chat among the coffee crowd.

Hector had the three get in the backseat but didn't tie them down until after he had driven a few miles from the church. He then pulled over.

"You," he said to Anna. "Take the rope and knot it around those two. Be sure to get the hands. All hands."

Anna did as he asked. Then Hector reached into the backseat and checked the knots then bound Anna's wrists similarly. He tested the knots twice more. Satisfied, he put his gun on the passenger seat, arranged himself in behind the wheel and drove back onto the street.

"Can I ask you something, Hector?" Anna asked.

"Don't call me Hector. That's not my real name."

"Well, what is your name?"

He glared at Anna through the rearview mirror.

"Okay. You are nameless. Nameless, can I ask you something?"

"Sure."

Outside, a small boy chased a dog, as three goats chased him. The boy was oblivious to the car as it rode by and left him in a blanket of dust, too invested in what seemed to be a well-rehearsed game of chase. William wondered about the man with the flask. He wondered where he was, how far down the rabbit hole he had fallen. A part of William wanted to be having a drink with him.

"How long have you been sober?"

"Three months."

"You don't strike me as a violent man."

Hector laughed.

"I'm sorry but you don't."

"You didn't know me when I was drinking. All three of you would be dead. Tortured first."

"Don't listen to my mother. I absolutely believe you're violent," Maggie said. "Drinking or not." Maggie hesitated. "That was supposed to be a compliment."

Anna ignored her daughter and continued to press Nameless. "But why do you do it? I watch the news. It all seems so senseless. Why? And don't say *money*. Find a better reason." She hadn't wanted to say a thing but she found the words escaping, like a well-intended arsonist with just one little match.

Hector reached for the gun and put it in his hand.

Hector stared straight ahead. Outside, a series of cloud vapors made a suspicious V in the southern sky. There wasn't a bird to be seen in the entire blue expanse. Hector used the gun to reposition his glasses upon the bridge of his nose.

William felt as though he could hear Hector's thoughts, even as the hemp rope bore into his wrist. William, who had spent so many hours interloping, overhearing the escaped words of strangers through their open windows, now imagined he could do the same with Hector's thoughts:

I was happy as a killer. I enjoyed the role of villain. It gave me power. Power is my ultimate drug. To watch someone wither at the very sight of you, at the smell of your sweat, is an elixir one hundred times more powerful than a kilo of cocaine. It's the presidency of vice, because everything lays prostrate in its wake. I was rising in the ranks. I was making my name known. I was doing everything I was supposed to be doing. Then something happened. It was this past summer, on the hottest day of the year in the middle of August. I woke in my bed, the mattress slick with sweat. I curled up like a dead insect and wrapped the sheet over my head despite the heat. I was overcome by a crushing loneliness. It was like a poem.

I slept for days on end. I couldn't move and it wasn't just the summer heat. I felt buried alive, like I was slipping into the ground. I wasn't long for this life, maybe I'm still not. I saw the end without really seeing it and it made me gasp and choke and nearly die for air. It scared me. It scared me sober and only then did I feel alive, did I feel as vital as breath.

And now I have no idea who or what I am. I am trapped in the middle of two versions of me, the villain with power and the man with breath and I don't know how in the hell I can balance each.

"To make money. There is no better reason," Hector said. "Now shut up. All of you."

The rest of the drive acted like a sedative. Anna stared silently out the window. Maggie had her eyes shut but wasn't sleeping. William longed for a stiff one. The miles rolled by. Hector whistled some tune, known only to himself, in a soft deep baritone that didn't assuage the soporific nature of the trip. The road that stretched forever.

William thought of Pedro. He smiled, remembering the grocery store clerk. Soon, he found himself thinking of Pedro's son. What did he look like? What did he do? What did he know of his father? How would he respond when William introduced himself to the young man? He realized he would need Maggie's help. She would have to accompany him to explain things. She would need to help him. He thought about this for a few moments and found a smile. Hell, at least he wasn't thinking about death or dying. This was progress.

Anna wanted to speak to Hector. She wanted to reform him. She wanted to tell him he was ruining her country. That the world viewed her Mexico like a mine field because of men like him. Bloated scarred drunks all of them, whether or not they were drinking. But she knew it was futile to protest.

Plus, he had a gun and though she didn't think he was a violent man, she knew not to test him. She had watched the news. Every night.

So, she stared out the window and thought of what needed to get done on her farm. The chilies and sunflowers would need harvesting soon and then it would be off to the market just north of San Luis Potosi to sell in bulk. Thank god for the van, she thought. That was going to change everything.

Thank god for William, she thought. I will show him my crops and let him run his hands through the soil, the one thing she could control. She continued to gaze out of the window and wait for all the nonsense to pass.

And then it struck her. What if Nameless takes the van? What if that is where they're going? If this van is good for hauling crops, it might be good for hauling, whatever it is men like Hector hauled. Breathe, she told herself.

Maggie had never felt younger. She felt like a child. Silly, in trouble, about to be punished for a sin she did commit but couldn't remember committing. She felt as though she had hives, though nothing itched.

"We're almost here." Hector said. Three sets of eyes shifted forward, towards the cab.

"Where?" Anna asked.

"To where we're going."

31

Hector steered the car down a dirt alley. The terrain was choppy. Recent rains had formed ravines in the dull orange dust and the truck barreled over each with considerable effort.

"Damn. I need Dramamine," Maggie said.

"I think the transmission is going on the van," Anna said, a little too loud.

William looked at her.

There were rows of shacks on either side of the alley. Tiny boxes masquerading as homes. Flat tires, broken wheelbarrows, tufts of dead grass rested on the cheap tin that served as walls. In between each house was a patch of dirt, bordered with fences in various states of ruin. Squawking chickens with faded orange feathers ran to and fro, looking like jaundiced kings. A laundry line held a tattered rag and a baby's blanket, both of which the wind was threatening to steal.

"Is this where we're going?" Anna asked, softening her tone.

"Yes."

"Can I ask why?"

Hector stopped the truck and pulled to the right of the alley. He sighed heavily and then turned back to the captives.

"I suppose I have to tell you. We are at an orphanage. Well, a series of orphanages really." He paused and wiped sweat from his brow. "I have a child here."

"In this place?" Anna said, her tone indicating just what she thought of the surroundings.

"Yes."

"But you're a man of wealth. Why on earth..."

"Mama," Maggie said.

"I'm sorry," Anna said.

"No. I will answer. I am a happily married man. I have three wonderful children. One is a student at Cal. Another has three restaurants in Mexico City. A third is finding himself somewhere with the Incas. He takes after his mother," Hector said, smiling for the first time since the abduction.

Hector continued. "I also have a fourth child. A little girl named Consuelo. She's seven years old. This is her home. She is the reason we are here today." Hector sighed again.

"Hector, why?" Anna asked.

"I have a wife. She is not the mother."

"Okay. So why must your little girl live here? You aren't the first man to have a child with a mistress."

"Because the woman who is Consuelo's mother is well known by my employers."

"You shat where you ate," Maggie said.

"No. That's not it. The child isn't normal." Hector looked at the horizon through the window. It was hard and straight as ever.

"What does that mean?" Anna asked.

"It's hard to explain but it is what it is. My little Consuelo lives here and I need you to help me ask her something. You can sign in LSM, right?" With the gun in his hand, Hector pointed directly at William.

William nodded.

Hector let them out of the van and untied the ropes from their wrists. Then he led them to one of the orphanages and knocked on the door, which quickly opened.

Three young women raced around the single room of the orphanage with the heaviness of nuns yet the quickness of mice. One moved a toy rattle from the floor to a small corner table. One scanned the floor for dust and debris. The third timidly approached Hector, her head down.

"Sir," she said. "I think we have a finger's worth of brandy."

"No, Marta. Thank you. I won't be having anything today."

The nuns stopped the whirling dervish activities and stole quick glances at each other.

"Hector, I swear these women are afraid of you," Anna said. Her boldness made Maggie nervous.

"Marta, where is 'Suelo?" Hector asked.

"Down the street. She is getting deloused."

"Ah. Well, let's see to her then."

Marta nodded and led the way out of the room and back down the ravine-riddled alley.

They came upon a group of ten children waiting in line. Most were shirtless, all were shoeless. Flies buzzed over the ubiquitous dog feces that blended in with the dirt. The children saw the group but didn't react. They were unnaturally quiet. They didn't tease each other, they didn't whisper secrets or kick *pelotas*. They stood there with pleasant half-smiles and just watched. A little girl sniffled passively.

William instantly liked them.

A woman sat on a three-legged stool at the head of the line. With a flattened wooden stick, she examined the scalp of a little girl, moving her fingers roughly through the coarse head of black hair.

"Paco," she said, "*ven acà.*" A boy peeked around the corner. He had a razor in one hand. He looked to be twelve or thirteen and had a tattered T-Shirt that said *Jawbreaker*.

"Si?"

"She's next."

"Consuelita!" Hector said. The little girl who was being checked looked up and saw her Hector. She broke free from the grip of the woman with the wood stick.

"No, Consuelo," the woman said, then she looked up at Hector. "She has lice. Paco, take her please."

Marta led them back to the single room to wait until Consuelo's treatment was finished. The two nuns were gone now, and, after opening the door for Hector, Marta disappeared as well.

"Hector, do you know anything about cars?" Anna asked.

"A little."

"I think that van has a carburetor problem."

William turned his head toward Anna.

So did Hector.

"Hector, have you ever been to Los Angeles?" Maggie asked, after an extended period of slightly uncomfortable silence.

"I have."

"Did you like it?"

"I found it tedious. I prefer life down here. I felt second class up there."

"I have been saying that for years," Anna said, forgetting about her attempts to throw the van under the bus. "You know how many I've lost to the red, white and blue?" Anna waited for a guess to come. "Eight. Eight of my family that I can only know through Sunday phone calls."

"You guys don't know," Maggie said, gesturing outside to the kids with lice crawling through their hair. "Most people spend their whole lives trying to get the hell out of here. It's the awful truth." Maggie pointed her finger for emphasis. "But it's the truth."

"It's your truth," Anna said. "I choose to stay and try make this place better."

"That's right, Anna," Hector said.

"Said the drug dealer."

"Maggie. Have some respect."

"And what do you think, William?" Hector asked, chuckling a bit.

William had lived his life like Anna, staying close to home. But he fantasized like Maggie, holding on to his one time in Palm Springs like the last nugget of gold. And he dreamed like Hector. Big, loud, bombastic dreams with guns drawn.

He shrugged.

A knock on the door interrupted their conversation.

"Come in," Hector said. The door squeaked open. A small shadow entered the room first, followed by a bald little girl. Someone had put her in a baby doll dress with a mustard stain across the chest and scuffed patent leather shoes. She gripped an adult-sized clutch. She looked like a child prostitute with leukemia.

"All better, now Consuelo?" Hector asked. She didn't move.

Hector looked at William.

"She can't hear or speak."

William motioned his hands to Consuelo. "How is your head?" He signed, his hands dexterous as they twisted and turned. He had to spell every word out in Spanish. She didn't understand American Sign Language. Bored, she rubbed her bare scalp. But after watching William twist his fingers this way and that, she finally smiled.

"She's lost teeth!" Hector said proudly.

"He says you've lost teeth?" William signed.

She looked at Hector and moved her hands from her scalp to the gap in her mouth where her teeth had been.

"Ask her how she's doing? Is she happy here?" William asked her. She looked at Hector then at William.

"It's okay," William signed. "I'm your friend. I love your bag." She smiled. "You know, I can't talk, either. You and me are a lot alike."

"But you're white," she signed nervously. Her hands moved slowly, forced and jarring. They were hands that stuttered. "Marta says that you only care about yourself."

"Marta's very smart. But I'm not like that. This man wants to know if you are happy."

"I was happy. But then something happened and now I'm not happy."

"What happened?"

"My dog ran away."

"Oh, no! Have you looked for him?"

"No. Marta says that dogs are pests that give us lice."

"Well, maybe the dog will come back."

"It's been five days."

Maggie watched as Consuelo and William traded flailing messages. She looked for patterns but couldn't find any.

"You know I had a pet run away from me once," William continued.

"Was he a dog?"

"No. Sammy was a bird. And she was a girl bird. A beautiful bird that could talk." Consuelo's eyes lit up. "Every morning she would say my name and wake me up. But she wanted to go on a great adventure up in the skies, so I let her go, even though it made me very sad. Maybe your dog wants you to go on a great adventure. And that's why he chose to leave you. So you wouldn't feel bad about leaving him behind."

Consuelo squinted her eyes, thinking about what William had just signed to her.

"Do you miss her?"

"William, what the hell are you two going on and on about?" Hector moved across the room to where William and the girl were standing.

"Listen," he said, whispering in William's ear, "I need to know how I can do something for her. Give her something. To make her feel better. It's part of my recovery."

William bent down and looked Consuelo directly in her eyes.

"Do you know that this man is your father?"

She nodded, very slowly. But she nodded.

"Well he loves you. And he wants to know what would make you the happiest little girl in the entire world."

Consuelo thought about this for a few seconds.

"New teeth. I miss my old ones," she said.

William smiled. "That can be arranged, if you don't mind waiting for a few weeks."

She didn't mind.

"What did she say?" Hector asked, when he was sure the two were done with their exchange. William motioned a pen and paper.

"In the truck," he said to Anna. When she returned William scribbled down Consuelo's request:

A new dog, new shoes, a lunch visit with you every Friday where we have chocolate and Cokes and I want you to kiss me on the forehead when you leave, like people do on TV.

"Okay, my 'Suelito, okay," he said. He walked over to his daughter and kissed her gently on the forehead.

32

W illiam let the wind hit him through the rolled-down window as Hector drove back to the small grocery store. Anna sat in the front seat. Maggie was in the back next to William. The hemp rope was on the floor and the gun was somewhere unseen. An odd friendship had formed somewhere on the road, or maybe in the church or the orphanage, but it happened and tied wrists seemed unnecessary.

"I feel like today was the first day I got to hear her voice," Hector said at some point, to no one in particular.

Later, William stuck his head out of the car window. He thought, right then, that dogs were geniuses. The wind seemed to erase the wrinkles and the gray. The wind seemed to rush eternal and William thought that this was the most perfect fucking day ever, this day with a blue sky and yellow sun and tufts of white clouds and birds like Sammy flying and circling and diving for food. William felt good. He felt it would be a day like today when his mouth would open and words would fall out of it, words that followed each other, in a perfect fluid line that started and ended in the order in which they should. Beginning to end, alpha to omega, young to old.

He didn't understand how just hours earlier he wanted to die.

"William?" Hector said, louder than he had the three times prior. William moved his head away from the wind tunnel.

"William. I can't thank you enough for what you did."

William smiled. He pointed at the paper and pen that was now on the floor next to Maggie. She handed it to him.

Hector, would you like me to teach you to sign? It's not very difficult.

"Hector, William wants to teach you how to sign."

"In an hour? 'Cause I'm dropping you off in an hour and then you all have to leave and I have to never see any of you again. To my men, you are all ghosts."

The father ebbed away as the General returned.

"Plus, I could never learn to use sign language. It seems too difficult."

Maggie took the pen and wrote something that she showed only to William:

All fathers are the same.

William put his head back out of the window as Maggie crumpled up the piece of paper and stuffed it in her pocket.

The grocery store was empty when they arrived. Dusk was settling in and a violent stretch of pink and purple clouds tattered the western sky. Hector was short with his goodbyes. A quick nod was all they were given. Maggie watched the man enter the store. She watched as his head floated along the half window. She watched him, that stoic face, disappear and she tried to hide the fact that her hands were trembling.

Maggie drove silently and had no idea if Anna and William had said anything to her or to each other. She gripped the steering wheel and though her eyes were open, she wasn't watching the road. Someone else was driving, someone else had entered her and was manipulating all the mechanics of living. She could feel her breath enter her nose and swirl around in her lungs. Her body was an empty rusted vat and she tried to recall the last time she felt joy. She tried to recall the last time that she felt anything but rust and the fear of rust. Then, she started to laugh. A laugh so severe she had to pull the van off to the side of the road to avoid swerving. The laughter built like a wave. It kept getting bigger and bigger and then it crested and fell quickly and violently. She sobbed and sobbed. Anna could do nothing but watch. William, in the front seat next to her, let her collapse into him and he gently stroked her hair as she wept.

"We could've been killed," she said softly. "We lucked out with Hector. If it had been anybody else, if it had been those men, if Hector wasn't in the back, if Hector had just one drink, if William didn't sign. We should have been dead."

"All the shit you've had to deal with, jail, whores, kidnapping? It seems fair to me." Maggie said to William, sometime after she had calmed down. Anna was sleeping soundly in the backseat.

William looked at her with a contorted face.

"You're an illegal alien coming into Mexico. It's supposed to be tough. It's not supposed to be easy." She slapped at his thigh playfully. "Do you know after I crossed into the States, I thought the hard part was over. That was silly of me, I know." She peered into the mirror to see if Anna was still asleep. Once she was sure of this, she continued. "Lupe, my cousin who came with me, and I were in a pickup truck with maybe twenty others, hidden in the camper of the truck, and we were just about to get into El Paso, where we had a safe house all set up to go to. A cop car passes us going in the other direction. Our driver, a white guy, eyes the cop in the mirror. He sees the cop car slowing down. The Mexicans are coming, the Mexicans are coming. That's what that cop was thinking. I remember seeing this look of absolute panic spread across our driver's face, I could paint that face right now and it would be a perfect replica. And then I remember he gunned the accelerator and my body lunged forward and then whipped back. I felt so slight. The siren was loud, even though the cop was a ways behind us. The man drove the truck off the road and into this abandoned field. 'Run' he told me, and then said the address of the safe house and pointed. He opened the back of the truck, the others piled out. I grabbed Lupe and we fucking ran."

Maggie was out of the breath. She was staring straight ahead in the darkness of the desert night. Then she laughed.

"Do you know what happened next?"

William shook his head.

"We scattered like a dropped bag of marbles, me, Lupe and some guy from Oaxaca who was chewing tobacco. He had that stupid pouch of shit in his lower lip and even as we ran, he chewed. We could hear the cop sirens getting closer to the field. I saw the others running, digging holes in the dirt to cover themselves, diving in thorny bushes. But, everyone was silent, like when you watch the Discovery channel and they show a rabbit being pursued by a fox in slow motion. Determined silence. The white man who drove us stayed by his truck. The truck was worth more than we were. From overhead, a beam of light was trying to track us. They had a fucking helicopter after us. Twenty poor – beyond poor – people who just wanted to pick fruit and clean toilets. Lupe and I ran the direction the man had indicated but I had no idea where the fuck the safe house was. There were more sirens back at the field now. It was just a matter of time before we were captured and put in jail where we belonged. The fucking helicopter had spotted us and was shining its light right on us, no matter how hard we tried to lose it."

Maggie stopped and laughed again.

"Then, it started to hail, if you can fucking believe that, it started to hail. These huge, golf-ball sized fuckers. It was like god was shooting spitballs at us. They hurt like hell. But it was worth it. The hail scared the helicopter away. We somehow made it. I found the house while in a fugue state, but I found it, damn it. That's the only time in my entire life I have ever seen it hail. Saved by hail."

William indicated he wanted more. He had never heard this story in all the years he'd listened to her and Lupe under their window.

"Nothing else happened. We stayed at the safe house. Had some food. Then my uncle picked me up a day later and drove to LA."

33

Maggie drove through the night without stopping. Anna slept the entire time. William tried his best to stay awake, only to fall asleep with his head pressed against the window. Once he was finally asleep, he was out for the duration of the night.

The sun woke Anna up. She yawned and stretched and then resumed her taciturn pose in the back seat.

"Morning, Mama."

"Morning. You didn't sleep?"

"No. I just needed to drive, to keep moving."

"Like a shark."

Maggie smiled.

"Like a shark. Let's stop and get some breakfast."

"Why don't we wait until we get home? It's not far."

"I know but once we get there it's going to be brothers and sisters and cousins."

Maggie looked at her mother in the mirror and smiled.

"Well, if a shark needs to eat, far be it from me to stop it."

William awoke in the front seat of the empty van. It took him a moment to get his bearings. The van was parked in a dirt parking lot. The shadow of a semi-truck loomed over it, blocking the sun. He spotted Maggie and Anna sitting in a small roadside diner. Maggie was drinking orange juice and nodding at whatever Anna was saying. It was right then that William realized that he hadn't dreamed anything during the night. It was a dreamless night and he'd slept with a peaceful heaviness that his father had always bragged about. "Out the minute my head hits the pillow, stay that way 'til the alarm goes off," he would tell his sons as he read the business section. As the driver of the semi rumbled the engine on, William became aware that he had an erection. The erection of a teenager and with a teenager's desperate need to do something with it. He felt it through his pants. He moved his hand away. It puzzled him. This hadn't happened in a very long time. And then he felt it again. It felt good. Maybe this was why his father was such an arrogant asshole. He waited for it to go down and then he got out of the van and went to join the women, kicking a rock along the way.

"William, my people have lived in my hometown for six generations," Anna said.

"I hate that expression – *my people*," Maggie said. "It feels so, I don't know. It feels like something a victim says."

"Enough," Anna said and Maggie put food into her mouth immediately.

"As I was saying," Anna continued, "my people have lived in my hometown for generations. We have a street named after us. It runs the length of the town, from the main square to the southern tip where the market place is."

"Everyone's had a ride," Maggie said and laughed at the joke she had endured since grade school.

"My great, great grandfather was a master carpenter," Anna continued, "and helped build the church that still stands today. *Iglesia de La Mujera de el Christo*. It's a beautiful building, I would love to show you it."

William nodded. She spoke of her town as one speaks of the sacred and the pristine, as if it resonated something more than a place to eat and work and live and die. He could hear the pride in each syllable, echoing from a congenital part of her and he thought it was magical.

"Mama, sorry if I don't share your reverence for Puebla. I just don't get why you're so proud of a place that offers nothing."

"And what has Los Angeles ever given to you? Famous people? That tattoo?"

"It's given me a job and freedom and the ability to do as I please. And money."

"Do as you please? What does that even mean? No one can do as they please except for a prince or two. In Los Angeles, you are still a bartender?"

"I am."

Anna yanked at the loose strands of silver hair that fell down both cheeks and dug them back behind her ears.

Maggie was about to respond but she stopped herself. She realized that things were back to normal now. Home was on the horizon. Hector and AA meetings and bald little girls were gone and with them the momentarily allied team of Anna and Maggie. Without the threat of a gun, without a masked man with villainous intentions to distract Anna, things slipped back to the way they had always had been. Maggie returned to her rightful role as dangerous renegade, as the daughter apostate whose damage to the family was pandemic in scope.

"We were a city made rich by gold at one point. It was like confetti in our river. Little specks everywhere. The Indians found it, knew where it was hiding once the river dried up and the Spanish sold it. But this ended two centuries ago."

And nothing has happened since, thought Maggie.

As they neared the outskirts of Puebla, Maggie felt nervous. Up until now, it had been easy to forget about this little town in the middle of nowhere. It was a country away. It was a two, three hour flight away. It was always a few days away. William helped. He was an ever-present distraction. But now it was here, without distraction.

Crude dirt streets lined with rocks. A dog tied to a post, thin with hunger. Old bicycles in the yards of rundown houses. Chain-link fences with frayed edges, oxidized and crumbling. It looked nothing but gray. She needed to say something to stop herself from mental flagellation. Her hands began to shake a bit but she didn't cry again. She breathed in and out and focused straight ahead. *I'll be gone in a few days*, a mantra voice intoned inside her head. And then to distract herself, she exclaimed in her steadiest of voices that everything looked so much smaller than she remembered.

William understood what Maggie meant. He wondered how small his own life back in LA would look when he returned. He was afraid it would be too small to even find.

"Well it's not. It's the same size," Anna said flatly. Then she pointed to a corner. "That was where the bus picked you up for school." Maggie didn't look.

"Make a left at the post," Anna directed, as they drove deeper into the town.

"I know where we're going," Maggie said.

They had driven past Lupe's house a mile back. Maggie thought of the late nights in Lupe's bedroom, speaking in a made up language so Lupe's two younger sisters wouldn't understand their talk of boys and beer, listening to American music on the cassette deck Lupe's father had sent from Texas. It wasn't all bad, she allowed herself to admit.

A few minutes later and after more directives from Anna, Maggie pulled into the makeshift driveway that led to a modest house. The house had seemingly been built in stages, as each wall was painted a different color, and was in various stages of decay and repair. A new window was conspicuously bright against a wooden wall that had been splattered by a rainbow of beige, tan, nude and brown paint. Part of the roof was caved in, but the swing on the large veranda that wrapped around the front seemed to be freshly stained mahogany, which tilted here and there. An old man sat in a rocking chair. He didn't seem to notice the new visitors, but kept a steady rocking. He wore the satisfied countenance of someone old enough to enjoy invisibility when and if he chose.

"This is home," Anna said.

Maggie walked into the living room expecting to find her siblings there. Instead, she found it empty of people. She turned and saw Anna walking William down the drive, most likely towards the farm.

She looked at the room, studied it. If the town itself looked the same only smaller, this looked the same only larger, bigger in scope than just the things that filled it. The recliner, solely her father's, had been the carpet ride she went on to find Aladdin, in those rare hours when her father wasn't asleep there, beer in hand, the black and white television reflecting glimpses of the football game. The sunflower curtains and the blanket that draped over the mauve sofa were both summer projects she and her sister Flora accomplished despite unbearable heat and Anna's constant criticism. The yellow was faded now, looked too much like spicy mustard but the brown had retained its solid hue. The dining table, just to the left of the main room, was always set with those pieces of fine silver and china (inherited from the one rich aunt in the family tree) that Flora and Lupe and Maggie would try and save from the incoming pirates played dutifully by brothers and cousins. Maggie let her fingers trace the gilded etching of the Bible that rested on the small round coffee table. She hated those nightly readings of John or Acts or Ephesians but the book itself, big and green and holding eternity in its endless thin little pages, was the only thing she truly feared. Except of course, for Anna.

She went to the hallway where rows of family portraits dwelled, nailed to a wall. Flora was old now. The lines on the edges of her eyes were visible even in the slightly sepia tone and Maggie knew that meant her own must be worse. And Flora had gained weight, always too indulgent. She had two kids, one of each. Maggie had no idea what their names were.

In the next picture was a grown-up Fatima, no longer with the perpetual snot nose, no longer saddled with semi-permanent conjunctivitis and hives and hay fever. She looked gorgeous in a tacky prom gown.

"You're back," said a soft voice.

Maggie turned and saw Flora. She wore a pair of ill-fitting jeans, too tight for the apple belly she now possessed.

"I am."

"Well, come give me a hug."

The sisters embraced as the wall of family watched. It was a quick hug. Maggie sat on the edge of the sofa and let her hands search for and find the sunflower blanket, squeezing it into her hands.

"How was the trip?"

"Long. Weird."

"You have an accent."

"Nah, I still sound like I'm from here." Maggie wrapped the blanket around her. "How are the kids?"

"Guillo and Beatrice? Fine. Getting bigger. Every day."

"Where is everyone?"

"The boys are off shooting or something. Auntie is at her place getting ready for dinner. I don't know. Everyone is out." Flora smiled and then looked away. "So, Fatima has Jessica in town doing some shopping. They should be home in a couple of hours."

Maggie heard the sentence perfectly, she understood each word by itself. Fatima: Sister she hardly remembered. Town: A place one lives. Shopping: An activity one does to purchase goods. Jessica: The daughter one abandons.

"Okay, okay," Maggie said. "Great."

"We're going to Auntie's at seven."

"Perfect." Maggie tried to find a watch that wasn't on her wrist. "Listen I need to go find William."

"Who?"

"The gringo who's giving Mama the van. He's probably lost. It's what he does."

Maggie rushed past Flora and thought she heard her sister whisper, "She must be on drugs again."

Anna was showing William the old truck that had been rendered useless. It was a big dead Toyota extra cab, up on blocks, the engine ripped out and in pieces over the yard, a massacre of metal.

"Without transportation we can't get our produce to the main market. We had this truck for almost twenty years. It's sad when things that once ran so smooth just sort of die on you."

William felt a bug land on his arm, a big black beetle that looked like a bruise on his white skin.

"You see over there?" Anna pointed to a patch of farmland. "That's our habanero chili acre. Those are getting big in the States. Many Texas grocers come all the way down here to buy them from us. Imagine that? And then we have huge sunflowers. William, they grow taller than you. We have jalapenos and basic bell peppers, too. My goal is to produce a hybrid. I'm learning all about it online."

William picked up a spark plug, then tossed it.

"Come with me," Anna said, and took him by the hand. She walked with him across her land, a half-mile trek, pointing out the history of the farm, how the irrigation had been installed decades earlier, the lean years when drought and lack of volition hurt the outcome, her undying trust in the land, the firm desire to keep it small and vital, to keep it localized and in the family and keeping the product fresh and pure. "You guys have organic up north but this is more than organic. It's mine," she said. William nodded and listened. As she spoke, he came to understand that he wanted to live like Anna lived.

After she showed him the rows of seed and plant, they meandered back to the house.

"You know, we're doing very well now that they shut down the huge produce plant just outside of town. Hell, what they threw away from spoilage was three times what we produce to sell. We could never compete with them but now, for the first time, I feel we have a shot." She stopped and took in the view of her land. "Just maybe a shot and we have you to thank. It's not just a van to me, William."

William reached over and took her hand. He held it in his own. Anna turned to him and for one moment, he thought he would kiss her. Instead, he brushed a loose strand of hair that had whipped against her face and placed it behind her ear. He mouthed the words, "You are welcome."

"Oh for fuck's sake," Maggie said as she came from behind the dead truck and saw William and his mother holding hands. "I mean for fucking Christ's sake."

Neither Anna nor William acted as if they heard her. William didn't let go of Anna's hand.

"William, I need you."

William didn't move.

"You two can play really awkward lovers later."

William didn't move.

"William, please."

Finally, he let go of Anna's hand and turned to Maggie.

"I'll bring your boyfriend right back to you, Mama." Maggie yelled to Anna.

Anna grabbed a piece of metal and threw it against the carcass of the truck. The ringing reverberated, but Maggie didn't look back.

"Someone should slap you right across the face."

34

Maggie drove the van back from where they came.

"I don't even want to talk about you and my mother. I just don't. You know she beat the fuck out of me, right? Keep that in mind, William. Do what you have to do, but I don't want to know." She drove faster than usual. They hit a pothole in the road and the van bounced up and down. "Shit. Shit." She pulled over right next to Lupe's old house.

How fucking dare she do this, whatever the fuck it is she's doing. William was sick of being in the van and he was sick of being with Maggie. He tried to open the door, but Maggie stopped him.

"No. We can't get out. This town is a time bomb and this van is, like, our haven. Don't ask me how the hell that can be true but it is, but it seems to be. It fucking protects us from shit. So, I need your help. Grab a pen and some paper. I need your help. Like how you helped that little girl."

William looked over at her.

"So remember way back when I told you that I was a shitty mother?"

William nodded.

"I wasn't kidding."

William nodded.

"Okay, so imagine that this is the day you get over your stutter. This is the day that you can finally speak."

William wrote something on the paper:

It would be the best day of my life.

"That's what you would think, wouldn't you? But what you wouldn't realize is that once you utter that first word, everything will change forever. Your entire universe will be altered. Maybe even in ways you never thought about. Maybe once you can speak, you don't know how to control it, so you just say whatever's on your mind without any reservations. You don't know tact or control. It would be a nightmare. The thing is, you can't go back after speech. Once you've said it, it's out there. Speech can be fucking deadly. Am I making any sense?"

William shook his head.

"I was ten when my father left my mother. I blamed her. I *blame* her. He left because he had important things to do, he was a spy. He needed to build or save a nation. That's what I told myself then. He left because he couldn't bear her, the gravity of her. That's what I told myself at fifteen. She was a rigid stone who didn't understand change and growth and progress and he needed to be free because it was dragging him down. That's what I told myself when I first got to LA."

Maggie looked out at the fence she climbed on during her lengthy tomboy phase. She'd push off any boy or girl who tried to climb up to dethrone her. "I know my dad is an addict lost to the Yucatan. I know he's a waste of space and time and energy. But that knowledge would've crushed me when I kid."

You're not your father.

"I'm worse, William. And I can't see her. I just can't. We're leaving right now and don't try to fucking stop me."

But William did try to stop her. He reached over and grabbed her hands, trying to pull them away from the keys in the ignition. She yelled his name. He didn't stop. He was thinking of Anna, what this would do to her, he was thinking of the dead Toyota and that strand of hair that would need to be brushed back again, sometime soon. And he was thinking maybe it was time for Maggie to see her daughter.

Maggie put up a struggle. She freed her legs from beneath the steering wheel and kicked William in the thigh. He reeled back but pounced up again. The battle was for the keys. Maggie held them in her left hand, using her right arm to fend off William as he grasped for them. The push and pull went on for some time until, without either of them noticing it, they were surrounded by three men just outside the van. Each had a tool – the first a large rock, the second a two by four and the third a metal pipe.

The man with the pipe, small and thin with wisps of undernourished facial hair above his lips, knocked the pipe against the passenger side window. William and Maggie stopped their fighting. The keys dropped to the floor of the van.

"What the fuck are you two doing?"

Maggie surveyed the scene and knew this could be trouble but couldn't find any words to explain. She glanced at William's door and saw that it was locked.

Then she looked closer at the man with the pipe. He looked familiar. He looked like someone from a photo she had lying in a box somewhere in her closet.

"Guillermo? Flora's Guillermo?" She asked quietly, too quietly for the man with the pipe to hear. The man with the rock, younger and heavier than the man with the pipe, went over to Maggie's door.

"Why don't you two just find someplace else to go at it?"

Maggie smiled at him. Benito. Little Benito was all grown up. And so big. And in front of her was Lou, holding a two by four. Of course Lou would be the one to remain inert. Silent Lou.

Maggie unlocked her door, with the biggest smile, got out of the van, and gave Benito a hug.

"What the fuck," Benito said, pushing her off.

"Benito. It's me. Maggie."

Benito peered into her as if she was the sun. He looked at Lou, who had already recognized her and was walking over.

"My god. You got old." Benito said.

"And you got fat," Maggie returned.

"Who's the old man?" Guillermo asked.

"Is that your white husband?" Benito asked. Maggie laughed.

"No. That's my neighbor. He's giving my mother this van. We drove it down here."

"Why? Why is he giving her his car?"

"He can't drive. He's a nice man. I don't really know. He just is."

"What were you two arguing over?" Lou asked, speaking for the first time.

"Which radio station to listen to. It doesn't matter."

William watched from inside the van as they did what people do after a long time has passed between visits. General pleasantries. Inquiries about mutual friends. Lots of overly excited transitions. At least this is what he assumed. What a funny little two-step, he thought, as the four old friends kicked up the dust.

"Bye guys. I'm sure I'll see you before I go. Say hi to your mother for me." Maggie said as she got into the van. The men waved at her. Each one gave William a quick glance over, before turning around and going into the house where Lupe had grown up.

"That was odd. Those guys were like my brothers when I was a kid," she said, watching them enter the house. "I had the biggest crush on Lou. Now he just looks old and is losing his hair. Aging is hard on memories."

William had taken hold of the keys while she and the boys caught up. He jangled them but kept them out of her reach.

"I have to do this, don't I?"

William nodded.

"Give me the damn keys and just shut up, William." William gave Maggie the keys and she turned on the engine.

35

Maggie gave William a quick driving tour of the small town. She showed him the main square in the center, the church her ancestor had built, the soccer field where she lost her virginity on an uncommonly cold night, the basketball court where she took the virginity of some boy who had access to tequila, the alley behind the main shopping street where the kids would hang out on Saturday nights, smoking weed and trying to get alcohol.

"I know I shouldn't do this but I want to drive past my daughter's father's house. He lives in North Carolina now but I just want to see it."

When they approached his house, she let out a sigh. It was in utter ruin. The roof had caved in, the windows shattered. The front door rested against the termite-rotted wood, unhinged.

"This is the home he promised for me when I told him I was pregnant." Maggie said and then drove away.

Anna and Flora were drinking tea when Maggie and William returned to the house.

"I showed William around town. And we ran into Guillermo. Why isn't he here?"

Flora sipped her tea and pretended not to hear.

"They're no longer together," Anna said. "Sit, both of you and have some tea." William sat next to Anna. Maggie sat down next to her sister.

"Flora, what happened?"

"It doesn't matter. Lupe is Guillermo's sister. I know how close you are to Lupe. I didn't want to put you in the middle of a bad situation." Then she took one more sip and excused herself.

Maggie didn't try to stop her. She just watched Flora, as if she was a character in a movie, walk towards the hallway and then disappear.

"I didn't know," Maggie said.

"Would you like more tea, William?" Anna asked.

William did not.

"Margarita, we will be having a little dinner for you at Auntie's. Just us, your sisters. Please be ready by seven."

"Mama, I want to talk to you about that."

"Yes?"

"Um, will Jessica be there?"

"Of course. She's family."

"Yes, she is. But maybe it might be best if she and I can first see each just the two of us."

"So we quarantine her off until you're ready to speak with her?"

"Please. Mama."

"Fine." Then Anna got up, collected the empty teacups and teakettle and went into the kitchen.

"Should've fucking left when I had the chance," Maggie said and then went upstairs.

William sat at the table. Why was it set, he wondered? He looked around the room. It was well lived in. The recliner had the faded cushion of extended use. The sofa, a soft purple, sagged in the middle. The armrests had turned almost gray by the endless forearms that had rested there over the years. He liked this room.

He fiddled with the polished silver fork. In some box in his garage he had silver forks and a silver candlestick. In boxes in his garage, he had his mother's worn Bible with Revelation heavily underlined and blankets she used to throw over a sofa or chair, possibly some curtains she had sewn when the moths got to the old ones. He had pictures of family outings, that summer in Kern for sure, pictures of his brother at the beach, his skinny white body dying for the sun, his brother's kids in Halloween costumes, a cowboy and a princess. He fiddled with a silver knife, too. Somewhere in his garage he had an old TV set that his father had watched Koufax dominate on, in black and white, oblivious to everything but the very next pitch.

Maybe, William thought, he would go and find these things once he got home. Just open up the garage and look in some boxes and see what was there to be salvaged. Maybe even take some of those things out of the boxes, out of the garage, and find a place for them.

William decided to explore the grounds a bit. He walked outside, past the old man in the rocking chair, who had dozed off and was snoring. He followed a footpath to the side of the house, past a shed that had lost its doors, past two broken push mowers–and a small flowerbed with the same red dahlias he'd picked in Juarez. He sat down against the nude-painted wall there and looked at the flowers. They needed water. He looked around for a hose or faucet but he couldn't find either.

Someone was singing from the window above him. It was Anna. She couldn't carry a tune, but kept singing anyway. William looked up at the window above him and felt compelled to leave. He picked himself up off the ground, went and picked a flower then went back inside the house.

36

"William," Maggie said in a quiet yell. "Get the hell out of that chair." William was asleep in the recliner. He lifted his head. "Get out. No one can sit in that chair. Not even my mother's new American lover."

William put his hands out to ask why.

"It was my father's. It's like his holy burial ground. Ridiculous, I know."

William slowly rose out of the chair and sat down on the mauve sofa.

"So, I think I'm just going to take Jessica aside and have a little heart to heart with her. Explain why it's taken me so long to come and visit. Take her for breakfast tomorrow and introduce myself to her that way. Does that sound like a good plan?"

William nodded. It did sound like a good plan.

He could tell that Maggie was nervous. She was trying to figure it out, but the twitch in her left eyebrow seemed to indicate she hadn't figured out anything.

"I think that's what I should do," she said.

Why anyone would ever have a child was beyond William's understanding. The weight of responsibility, the burden of guilt from the pain all parents cause, with or without intention, seemed too much to bear. A bird was hard enough.

Anna and Flora came in from the kitchen. Anna smiled at William and Maggie and then she let her eyes shift to the recliner. She stared at it for a moment and then shifted her eyes back to the sofa. William thought he detected a faint smile flash quickly across her face.

"You two ready?" Anna asked.

The foursome drove in Flora's Honda Accord. William recognized the Tejano music that played on the radio. How quickly he was becoming an expert.

"God, it feels good to not be driving," Maggie said from the backseat. "I feel like my life has been one big blur for the past week now. One big blur with my hands attached to a wheel."

Had it been a week? It felt so much longer to William.

They drove the rest of the way in silence. William liked being surrounded by women. There was something soft about it but a complicated softness, a softness that could burn and sear like a branding iron if one wasn't careful. But mostly he liked being near Anna. He wanted to reach through the seat and place his hand on the small of her back and let it rest there. He wanted to hear her speak of her farm with a passion he had never had for anything in his own life. He wondered if all those years of eavesdropping under Maggie's window somehow prepared him for this moment, riding in the back seat of a sedan with three Mexican women. He placed his hand on the seat in front of him, on the exact spot he imagined corresponded with the small of Anna's back. He let it rest there, pretending there was nothing between them except skin.

"Damn," Anna said. She dug in her purse for something.

"What?" Maggie asked.

"Auntie called me right before we left and said she had to go into town for some last minute errand and to bring my set of keys, but I forgot them."

"So. We'll wait. It's a nice night."

"We're not waiting," Anna said.

"Why? What's the point of driving all the way back to get keys when Auntie will be here soon enough?"

"Because then Maria will know I forgot the keys."

"You did forget the keys."

"I did. But there is no reason Maria needs to know this."

Maggie looked at Flora. Flora looked at Maggie. They both rolled their eyes.

"We will go back and get the keys. Then we will drive here and William will take the blame for us being late. We will say he overslept and he will agree. No one will mention the keys that were, I admit, forgotten. Okay?"

Soft like a branding iron, thought William.

37

Later, in the Honda, she would tell William that she should have seen it coming, which would remind William of that day in Sire's Grocery store when Pedro was killed. He should have seen that coming, too.

Her brothers, generally lazy young men who didn't have much ambition, were all away on some epic shooting desert adventure. Her cousins all missing, too. Only Uncle Arturo, almost comatose on the veranda, was present but diabetes, senility and incontinence always kept him close, so he didn't really count. The signs were all there.

They pulled into Anna's drive and Anna asked Maggie to get the keys, telling her they were on the kitchen sink by the mixing bowl. When she ran inside, she was met with a horrific reality.

William knew that Maggie, who performed secret monologues when she thought she was alone, who painted pictures of emaciated women of color and then set them on fire late at night in her bedroom, who was tough, reptile tough, let herself cry to the right pop song if the mood was just right but hated for anyone to see her exposed or vulnerable or not ready for whatever it was that was coming her way. He knew that she would absolutely hate, loathe, abhor, anything resembling a surprise party. And yet, as she opened the door to find her mother's keys, there it was. The unmistakable frenzied yells and screams: "Surprise!"

They had put up streamers and signs welcoming home Maggie. Food was on the table, as was the obligatory cake. In the kitchen, margaritas were being poured. Little kids ran wild with shrieks and giggles. William sipped a drink and watched the chaos. He noticed the three men from earlier that day now dressed in black dress shirts with mother-of-pearl cufflinks and bolo ties, their hair greased back tight against their heads. The one named Guillermo kept watching Flora but made no attempt to go to her. The one named Lou kept his eye on Maggie as she played politician, shaking hands, kissing babies, giving cousins votes of confidence for a life choice.

Everyone was there who was supposed to be there. Her brothers greeted her with backslaps and then went to find beer. Her sister Fatima wept openly when they hugged. Flora stayed in the corner and ate the dip.

"Isn't this great?" Anna asked, sidling up to William.

William nodded.

"I know she hates things like this but I couldn't not have a party. A big party with everyone here. I had this planned the minute I heard she was actually coming. I've been waiting for this for fifteen years. Look at her," Anna said, as Maggie tousled a young boy's hair. "And if I had told her about this, she would've found a way to back out."

William knew Anna was right.

"Can I tell you a secret?" Anna leaned in to whisper in William's ear. She led him outside, away from the eyes of her sons and family. They leaned against the van.

"I wasn't in Juarez to stop a niece from entering the US. I was there for a conference on seed hybrids. I had bus fare. I just wanted to see her on my own, before the family, before this night."

William cocked his head.

"It's no secret Maggie and I have had our differences but I wanted to spend time with just her. And you. But that was by accident."

William could smell the tequila on Anna's breath. He wanted to kiss her more than he had ever wanted to do anything in his life.

"Why are looking at me that way? I wanted you to know the truth. I didn't do anything wrong." Anna moved away from him. "I want what's best for my family."

An hour into the party, there was a knock on the front door. Anna, drunk, hushed the party.

"Maggie, *mi amor*, please go and answer the door."

Maggie was near Silent Lou, doing her best to drink away the awkwardness of a roomful of familial strangers.

"Me?" She asked, as she wiped away lime residue after drinking a shot. "Sure." She playfully punched Silent Lou in the arm and the two laughed at the same untold joke. As she walked towards the front door, everyone stopped talking and watched her. She looked at them suspiciously. "What?" she asked. "What?" she asked again, as she got to the door.

Your daughter is out there and you are too drunk to realize it, thought William.

But William was wrong. She opened the door and there was Lupe, Monster and Maggie's uncle.

"Surprise," all three said in English.

"We figured since you drove all the way down here, we had to at least fly down and see for ourselves if you actually made it," Tío said.

Maggie found she couldn't react. She stood there, gently pushing the door to and fro, watching these three figures that represented Los Angeles, standing on the threshold of her home in Mexico. It felt like the blending of two dissonant constructs, a particle and a wave, the ocean and Everest. Finally, the odd silence of the room forced her into motion and she went to Lupe, her oldest ally, and hugged her.

Monster grabbed her away from Lupe and kissed her on the mouth.

The party cheered this, but not Silent Lou. He had other plans for himself and Maggie but he kept those plans, and the effect of the disruption, to himself and in doing so he remained true to his moniker.

Maggie lost herself to the party. She drank more and more. Anytime she felt exposed by the strange amalgamation of persons, Lupe and Flora in the same room, Lou and Monster, William and Anna, Tío and Monster, her brothers and Lupe, Guillermo and Lupe, she drank. When she realized that her mother was witnessing the American version of her daughter, right before her eyes in her Mexican house, Maggie drank more. Soon, she wasn't the slightest bit upset at the surprise anymore. She grabbed Lupe by the arm and they danced and laughed like soldiers on the night of victory. She careened out of control.

Maggie didn't notice Flora watching the two carry on, digging more and more tortillas into the seemingly endless dip. Nor did she see Guillermo and Flora avoid each other the way a couple does just after a breakup. And Fatima, the kid sister she barely knew, kept going upstairs, coming back downstairs weeping, then back upstairs. Her uncle tried to talk about the bar but she pushed him away. She didn't care. She went from Lupe to Silent Lou and back again to Lupe, forgetting Monster was watching all of this, forgetting that she had told him she loved him seven days ago.

William spied on her the way he had done for fifteen years. From afar, from beneath a window, even as he sat out in the open on the mauve sofa. He wondered if she would ever stop this. He wondered if he ever would stop, too.

He attempted, in the din of the party, to open his mouth and say something to her, to put an end to all of it, as if he knew what all of *it* was exactly. He just knew everything seemed off, earthquake weather. He tried to open his mouth and speak to Maggie like he had to Hector's girl. He had things to say, things to say that might help her. He wasn't dead, he wasn't a ghost and he wasn't a fumbling old man who had never left Fountain Avenue.

He would let her know that things had changed, that it might be their turn to shine and that Mexico, just maybe, was ready to burst. And that mothers and daughters, like mothers and sons, don't have to engender only pain. They can be part good. Like holding hands in an AA meeting in the middle of nowhere. Good things.

But when he opened his mouth to speak, just as Maggie and Lupe sang the lyrics to an early Madonna hit that played on the stereo, all that came out was the warbled syllables that he was so accustomed to – ba, ba, ba – over and over, stripped of any beauty, a fumbling jeremiad lacking a moral.

"Ba, ba, ba," he said, and then kept repeating it, until it formed a song by accident. A toneless song with no chorus and no refrain. No one heard him do this. No one heard him stutter the last line of a goat song.

Later, when Anna came and sat down by him, he didn't reach for her hand.

"I feel like a teenager," she said to him, not realizing his lack of action. "I feel like everything is just as it should be."

Then you don't feel like a teenager, William thought.

And then he grabbed her hand in spite of himself, because he didn't know what else to do and because he loved the way it felt.

Maggie had gone outside to the shed to get ice from a standing freezer there. She sang "Papa Don't Preach" as she lifted the heavy lid, then reached inside and searched for a bag of ice.

"So this is where you grew up? The house of horrors."

She jumped when she heard Monster's voice.

"Fuck. You scared me," she said, holding a bag of ice.

"Sorry. So this is home?"

Maggie closed the lid of the freezer. She knew her smile was fake but donned it anyway.

"This is it. Where all the magic happened," she said, as he walked over to her and took the bag of ice. He leaned into her and she could feel his hard dick.

"I've missed you," he said.

She nodded. She wasn't a good liar. She knew that.

"Is there a place we can go?" He took her hand and placed it on the front of his jeans.

"I don't think so, Monster. It'd be weird."

"We've fucked on the cross-town bus."

"I know."

"Who is that guy?"

"What guy?"

"The guy you were doing shots with when I knocked on the door."

"Lou's an old friend."

"You and I were old friends before we got together."

"We were."

Monster put the bag of ice down on the ground and backed away from Maggie.

"You know, I've never been to Mexico. Fucking crazy. I have a Mexican flag tattooed on my fucking back but I've only ever gotten drunk at some TJ titty bar with more white boys there than all of Long Beach. When Lupe called and said we should all come down and to get the whole family together, finally, I was excited, you know? The homeland." Monster waited for a response. "Maggie, I came all the way down here."

"I had no idea this was happening."

"I came all the way down here, Maggie."

"I didn't know this was happening, Monster."

Monster took a couple of steps back and watched as the ice began to drip from the bottom of the plastic, hitting the ground like a metronome.

"Neither did I, Maggie."

"I meant the party. Why are you guys even down here, anyway? If you and Lupe and Tío were willing to come down, you guys should've driven down in the damn van."

"You were supposed to come down. It had been too long."

"Stop talking, Monster."

And he did. He chugged his entire beer, threw the can into the yard and walked back inside to rejoin the party. Maggie followed him, but not too closely, and left the bag of ice to drip slowly between the wood slats of the small shed.

Maggie reentered the house just as Anna had climbed up on the recliner to give a toast or speech. Monster went to Maggie's uncle, whispered something in his ear and left out the back door.

"Please, please. I want to thank all of you for coming," Her words slurred slightly and she stood unsteady on the recliner, a thin kite against a mild wind. "What a joyous day to see my family all together." She stopped herself and bit her cheek to stop the tears. "It's been fifteen years since I have seen my beautiful *hija* and here she is, right in front of me. It's also been fifteen years of separation for another mother and daughter. Two people close to my heart. Maggie, I want you to meet in person, Jessica." Anna swept her arm towards the stairwell. Fatima wept harder. Flora put down her chips. Coming out from the shadows of the hall and onto the landing, stood a sullen, slender girl of fifteen with dark chocolate hair and the round face of her mother.

Maggie saw her instantly.

She was wearing a *quinceñera* gown, a bit too small for her, with a plastic tiara on her head and too much makeup. Her vacant stare and crossed arms over breasts that seemed newly large, made it obvious that this wasn't her idea.

Maggie let the beer she was holding slip from her hand. She was watching herself. The beer spilled on the carpet, on her shoes.

"Come, come, Jessica," Anna urged. Maggie detected a slight eye roll from her daughter and she found herself doing the same thing.

Jessica made her grand cinematic movie entrance with unsure steps. She wasn't the dress-wearing kind, nor was she accustomed to the black pumps that impeded her gait. Jessica grabbed onto the railing tighter with each step.

Maggie couldn't run or scream or even truly comprehend why this was happening. She dug her fingers into her arms. She kicked the empty beer bottle away.

When Jessica's descent was final, Anna, who had since stepped down from her podium, went to Jessica and led her to Maggie.

"Jessica, this is your mother, Maggie this is your daughter, Jessica. Face to face. More than just a voice through a phone."

Maggie and Jessica stared at each other.

Then, Maggie turned to Anna, opened her hand and gave her a vicious, stinging face slap. That was the end of the surprise party.

38

Even after everyone had left and everything had been cleaned, Anna couldn't stop finding things to wash. She walked the house in a loop, looking for hidden dishes, trash, anything. William sat on the mauve sofa and watched her perform this ritual. Flora was still in the dining area, looking for dip.

"I made a mistake, didn't I?" She asked.

He nodded.

"No, you didn't, Mama." Flora chimed in. "You did what needed to be done."

"I thought it would be special," Anna said, ignoring Flora. "I thought it would help break the ice. She said she'd see her but I know she had Fatima keep her away all day. I just want things to be right."

William shook his head.

"Mama, you did the right thing. Do you hear me?"

"Not now, Flora. Please."

Flora wiped some crumbs off the table and flattened out her shirt then pulled it down over her large, round hips. The hips led her out of the room, growing wider and wider as she disappeared down the hall.

"What should I do?"

He shook his head no. Then put one hand over her mouth.

He nodded.

She nodded, too.

Then he leaned in and kissed her.

"We slept five to a bed. Every morning we woke up with the rooster," Anna said. Her bedroom was everything William had hoped it would be. Small. A desk cluttered with paperwork. Curtains cutting off the window from the world outside. A large bed with magenta sheets. He stood in the corner. She sat on the edge of the bed. She wasn't smoking a cigarette, but it felt like she should be. Confessionals mean more under the threat of smoke and fire.

"My younger brother was the man of the house after my father died of dysentery. He drank the first cup of coffee. If we had any. I remember watching him drink it, sitting on the table, looking out at our small farm as if it was a vast kingdom. When he finished, we ate our breakfast."

William had seen Anna's kingdom-viewing look when she described her small farm, too.

"Then we did chores," she continued. "Playtime was reading the Bible. Schooling was reading the Bible." Anna laughed. "My kids never had to read the Bible. Sure, I scared them with it. But that didn't work. Obviously." She stretched out her body on the bed. William then sat on a chair at the foot of the bed. He thought the room smelled of something green, like juniper or evergreen, though he couldn't be sure. "I gave my children their own rooms. I gave them a television. God, I remember the first time we watched *Sesame Street* together. Maggie loved the Oscar trash guy. She wouldn't miss that show. She'd wake me up three hours before it was on and whisper in my ear, 'is it time, Mama?'"

No, thought William, it's more of a red scent. It had a pepper hint to it. He was desperate to know what the scent was.

"I feel like she's been stolen from me." These words wafted out of her, dreamy and weepy and William could see her larynx pushing the words out like a baby blowing bubbles.

She is feeling sorry for herself, thought William. And like her love of dogs, it softened her. Her sorrow made her bendable and him needed, it stripped away the years, the wrinkles, and she seemed almost too young to touch.

As usual, he could not comfort her with words of distraction, with words that said nothing has been stolen forever, that waking up with brothers and sisters next to you is far better than waking up alone, so he rose up from his chair and laid down next to her.

He put his arm over her shoulder and brought her to him, slowly, allowing her to adjust to this. He resisted the urge to judge his actions, to critique the position of his arms and chest. He just let it happen the way it happened, no premeditation. She scooted over to him until her head rested on his shoulder and then she quit feeling sorry for herself and her mouth quit emitting dreamy, weepy words.

And then he thought her scent was fruit, guava, maybe even a hint of fresh mint.

39

—

Maggie woke up to the sound of Lupe's quiet snores. It was still dark outside. She could hear coyotes howling in the nearby canyons. She thought of the devil and then she closed her eyes again, waiting for sleep to overtake her, but it refused. Quietly, she climbed over Lupe but then lost her footing when her feet hit the ground. She fell hard to the floor.

Lupe woke, startled.

"What the hell?"

"Sorry, Lupe. I tripped."

"What time is it?"

"Early. I don't know. I was gonna make coffee."

"Make some for me, too."

Maggie and Lupe sipped coffee in the kitchen, both still in pajamas. They didn't speak at first. Just swirled more and more cream into the strong brew. The darkness and the early hour seemed to inspire the need for silence.

Then Lupe told a small joke about their Uncle (he smelled like pickled sorrow, was her punch line). Then she commented on something her husband had said last week (he believed in God and hoped she did too). Maggie then recited their favorite line from a movie they both loved (MAGGIE: "Ladies, you work on commission right?" LUPE: "Yes." MAGGIE: "Big mistake. BIG mistake. Huge.") Then Maggie said she wondered what happened to Monster. Lupe shrugged and said he'd be fine.

Finally, midway through their second cups, Lupe said it:

"Are you gonna see her before you go?"

Maggie smiled and poured Lupe a third cup of coffee and just then the sun peeked over the horizon and made a laser that cut right through the kitchen window.

* * *

William couldn't help but smile as Anna made eggs and chorizo. He tried not to, he tried to sit calmly, especially when Maggie's brothers began entering the dining area from all pockets of the house, like ants in a colony. They eyed him suspiciously but didn't speak. They grabbed plates and waited in a makeshift line for Anna to dish them food. He counted five in all. Five boys and three girls. His family was a skeleton compared to this. It was intimidating to him and for once he was glad he didn't have to try and speak to them, try to learn who each one was. He had Maggie, and now he had Anna and that was more than enough. Besides, he thought, they all had secrets, secrets no one would ever know. Because these men didn't talk. Ever.

Anna brought him his breakfast. She sat down next to him. She looked directly into his eyes. He looked back.

"Eat. Before it gets cold."

40

"You can ask me anything you want."

Jessica didn't say anything. She sat on Fatima's couch and stared at the ground with the hard, stoic dispassion so common in angry teenagers. Her hair covered her face. She had written on her jeans with a sharpie *blessed by the beast*. Maggie tried to find the meaning in that but knew better than to ask when she could not.

"You really hate me."

Jessica didn't respond.

"It's okay to hate me."

"Did you hate grandpa?"

"No. I envied him. He got out."

"Men really do get all the breaks."

"Please don't tell me you know anything about men."

Jessica laughed and then she stopped laughing.

"Did you save the letters I mailed to you?"

"Some of them. I saved the money. Well, I spent the money. But that's sort of like saving it. The rest of it, the letter itself, I just throw out."

"Why did you shut me down when I called?"

"I thought I was asking the questions."

"That's not an answer. Why wouldn't you talk to me?"

"I had better things to do."

"Your anger will go away."

"After I slap you in front of the family?"

"She lied to me and tricked me."

"I know. They did the same to me. I was holed up in that room for two hours trying to find a way to escape."

"Listen, I just want to tell you I'm sorry."

Jessica laughed. "You left to the States to make money for you and for me. Well, we do okay here. We don't need your money. So why don't you come home?"

"Because my home is there now. Why don't you come with me?"

"So I can live like a fugitive in a land that hates us?"

"They don't hate us."

"I guess you don't watch the news in LA."

"You've been talking to your grandma too much."

"Who else am I supposed to talk with?"

"You might like it. Los Angeles."

"Ooh, can we do mother daughter things? Get manicures? Facials?" Jessica clapped her hands with faux excitement.

Now Maggie laughed. "If you didn't hate me so much, you might really like me."

"I don't think so."

"Sure. We could Skype over lunch every Friday. And mock each other. Nothing would make me more proud. Then I could kiss the screen where your forehead is, like mothers do to their daughters on TV."

"What shows do you watch on TV where mothers do that to daughters?"

"It's just an option."

"There are lots and lots of options," Jessica flipped her bangs up from out of her eyes. "You don't really want me to come to Los Angeles and I don't really want to go."

Maggie rubbed her stomach, trying to find an itch.

"Let's say we get some lunch," Maggie said, finally.

"Not really that hungry."

"Oh, come on. Let me make you a sandwich. What does Fatima have here? Anything good?"

Jessica took her into the kitchen, where they found some carved turkey and mayonnaise and white bread. Maggie made the sandwiches and Jessica poured two Cokes. Then they walked outside to a small porch and sat down and ate lunch together without saying another word.

41

William didn't want to leave Anna's bed. They had just finished a nap. He heard her in the shower and thought he should join, let the water run down their bodies and nuzzle their necks, let the steam reheat the two of them, but he didn't. What if it wasn't her? What if the thrusts and the pulling of hair and the soft moaning had destroyed her, had destroyed them both? He was afraid to move.

She came from out of the shower with her hair wrapped in a towel. He breathed a sigh of relief. She was okay.

"I've printed out the directions you asked for," she said.

William nodded.

"I wish I could go with you. But I need to get some of the harvest to the market."

William smiled. The idea of a harvest seemed so wonderfully old fashioned.

She sat down on the bed, her robe closed tightly, and undid her towel, using it to dry off the wet strands of silver. William put his hand on her knee and squeezed it.

"William," she said, and she didn't need to say anything more.

William was already sitting in the passenger seat of Flora's Honda. Maggie watched him through the front window as he adjusted the mirror.

"He looks different," Maggie said.

"Who?" Flora asked.

"Doesn't matter," she said, and walked over to Flora. "Thanks for letting me use your car. I can't drive that van one more minute. We'll be back later today. Shouldn't take too long."

"It's fine," Flora said.

"Mama's gone?"

Flora nodded. Maggie took an apple from a fruit basket on the kitchen table.

"I think you should make it work with Guillermo."

Flora smiled. "Why?"

"Because," Maggie said. "I like you two together. It gives me hope."

"I keep thinking that maybe there is someone out there better."

"That's dangerous," Maggie said.

"I know."

"Call him, Flora."

"Maybe I will."

"Did you talk to Jessica?"

"I did." And then Maggie walked out of the house and went to the car where William was still playing with the mirror, sending fits of light beaming skyward from various directions.

42

"It feels strange to be back on the road. Like we already ended the trip and now it's starting again."

It did feel like that, William thought.

"At least we're not in the van."

Anna had the van and she and the boys were loading it with cut sunflowers. The van was no longer William's, which given what happened last night, was the best trade he could possibly think of.

"So, we'll go and meet your friend then drive back up and then take off tomorrow for the airport. Flora said she would drive us." Maggie was wearing new sunglasses, taken from Flora. They were thin with faux lizard skin frames and looked odd against her round face. She accelerated the small car into oncoming traffic. "Finally, something with a little pick up."

William had Pedro's wooden rabbit's foot in his hand. He rolled it over and over. He reached into his bag and pulled out his journal. He flipped through the pages.

Pedro is lost without Luis, his eldest son. I heard him weeping, sitting outside on a hot day, the hottest this August, so his window was wide open. No screen either and it was strange to hear a man like Pedro weep. He never cries and yet here he was, crying to his girlfriend. He worries about him, his Luis. He calls him a sensitive boy. I want to ask about him, Luis, the next time I see Pedro, tomorrow at the store, but how can I? How can I let him know that I hear him, that I understand...when I don't understand and when he can't know I hear him weeping?

Maggie smacked her gum. William closed his journal.

"You have the address?"

William nodded and handed Maggie a sheet of paper from his pocket.

"Luis Mendez. And with directions," Maggie said, after reading the paper. "Great. Should be quick and easy."

The tire blew twenty minutes into the trip. Maggie pulled the car over to the shoulder.

"Are you fucking kidding me?" she said as she and William assessed the damage. Shards of black rubber lay strewn over the pavement. There were no cars on the road in either direction. Maggie pulled out her cell phone and called Anna, Fatima, Flora. None answered. "Fuck," she said. When she and William discovered there was no spare, she said it a few more times.

"Let's walk to the nearest exit and see if we can find a tire shop or gas station or something."

William nodded.

Cars whirred past them and the dust kicked up and swirled, causing Maggie to cough.

As they walked, William suddenly remembered that Monster was at the party last night. What happened to him? He snapped his fingers to get Maggie's attention. When he had it, he mouthed the word MONSTER.

"I don't know. What a disaster. He and my uncle are staying a week at my uncle's cabin. Monster thought I would go with them, I guess." Maggie shook her head. "Why was he even there? Why were any of them? Shit, if they were coming down, why didn't they drive the van down to begin with? I mean, I loved seeing Lupe. She's flying back with us, by the way. I don't know."

They walked on. More dust. More coughing.

"She's pretty awesome," Maggie said, though she wouldn't look at William as she did.

William looked at her and mouthed LUPE?

"No, Jessica. I'm glad I came," she said. And then quieter, she said it again.

William thought of his mother the double speaker.

After walking to the main drag of a small town, they found a mechanic who had a spare for sale.

"I can drive you over and fix if for you but one of you will have to watch the store in the meantime. No one should come in. No one ever comes in."

"Except us."

"Except you," he said.

William decided to stay behind, since whoever went would have to drive either the tow truck or the Honda back to the shop.

The mechanic locked up the front of the store. "It's getting hot, gringo. Go stand in the shade. If anyone comes by," he pointed to the side of the small shop, "don't let them leave. Tell them I'll be right back. Deal?"

William shook the mechanic's hand.

"Be back in ten," Maggie added. And then the mechanic and Maggie climbed into a tow truck and drove away.

I am writing this to you, Luis Mendez, on the day after your father was murdered by a gang of drug-addled thugs in broad daylight. My name in William Thornton and your father was my best friend. I miss him very much and I always will. I have it on good authority just how much you meant to your father. You meant everything to him. I couldn't save him. I fear because of that fact, you will never know this truth, the truth of his love for you. To prove this, I am bringing you this letter, plus this small wooden rabbit's foot that your father kept for good luck. He always had it with him and, as he lay dying, asked me to come down here and give it to you. I am so sorry for your loss but know you are eternally loved.

William Thornton.

William hadn't reread his note to Luis since he'd left Los Angeles. He hated it. It was a lie. Pedro hadn't said a word to him about Luis, because Pedro was dead before William reached him that afternoon in the grocery store. William had stolen Pedro's life through a windowsill. He had stolen

Luis's address from a letter Pedro mailed years earlier, back when Pedro still lived in apartment eight. He wanted to be back with Anna, her smell of chili peppers (or was it guava and mint?) and strong coffee and sex. He tried to remember Pedro. He was short. Peaches and whiskey. He remembered that. Why was he doing this? This little wooden rabbit's foot, worn down from dark mahogany to a dirty honey color, this silly note, both soon to be handed over to some stranger he had never met. He shook his head.

The mechanic's truck pulled into the drive. William looked for Maggie to drive up behind him, but she didn't come. Probably went to get water, thought William.

"Thanks for watching the place," he told William after he pulled in and parked. William, still holding the note, felt as if he was exposing some secret as he stood in the sun with the paper flapping a little in the dry wind. The mechanic stared at him.

"What's the note?"

William shrugged. He didn't know what the note was. All he could think of was Anna and the farm. William stood in the sun as the mechanic stared at him, and he realized that everything had changed. That Pedro and Luis and this whole trip had changed its thesis. It wasn't about Pedro and his son. It was about Anna. He wanted to be back with Anna. He wanted to help her plant habaneros and sunflowers. The note felt heavy and false. He folded it and put it in his pocket.

"Whatever," the mechanic said, and went to reopen his store.

One more hour, William told himself. He would do this last favor, a eulogy to his old life in that little apartment listening to people through open windows. Then he would tell Maggie he wasn't going with her back to LA. He was staying in Mexico.

The Honda came peeling into the driveway fifteen minutes later. Finally, William thought. He had begun to worry. His immediate sense of relief was quickly replaced by a feeling of dread. She was driving fast. Something was wrong, William knew. She was driving too fast. She drove the car right for him as his thoughts remained on Anna and her citrus scent. Or was it the smell of desert sage?

She stopped the car a few feet in front of him.

In her hand was his journal.

It was open.

"What the fuck is this!" She yelled.

William the Life Stealer.

William the Liar.

William the Interloper.

(Nicknames his college roommate would have enjoyed.)

But he wasn't! The author of those entries was a different person. William, who had just found what he was looking for, who had migrated from suicidal mothers and stutters with endless syllables, from the death of a bird and a friend, to Mexico, where he battled ghosts and mimes and addicts and orphans. Where he had to endure all that shit so that he

might have one night in bed with a woman with
silver hair that clung to the side of her face. And now
he was exposed by his own words, written in black
ink with careful, plodding handwriting his first
grade teacher had complimented so often.

"You pervert."

But he wasn't, he wasn't at all. He wasn't now
and he wasn't then. He was caretaker, he was
guardian. He was what he always wanted to be: a
version of himself that didn't exist anywhere else,
those nights with the windows open. When others
wanted to send Maggie home, fuck her, leave her,
bruise her, mock her, he wanted to merely listen.

"You fucking liar."

How does someone who doesn't speak, lie?

"I feel sick, like I need to shower for years, you
dirty old fucking man."

Don't shower. Maybe it was Maggie he was
worried about that morning, maybe she would
finally collapse in on herself and swirl down the
drain.

"How often were you watching me? Did you
ever watch me change or fuck?"

No, never. Not once.

"Well you wrote down each time I had sex. Shall
I read a few passages? How about when I was late on
my period? How the fuck would you even know
that? You took stuff that was mine and made it
yours."

William shook his head.

"And now you're fucking my mother. Right?"

William walked towards Maggie. She was calm and poised, always at her best when she was angry and righteous. The mechanic was watching from inside his shop.

William went to her and took the book from her hands. Then he put his fingers to his mouth and instructed her to be quiet.

"Don't you tell me to be fucking quiet!"

William had no way of explaining. He walked to the trashcan by the front door of the shop and tossed the journal inside.

He walked back to Maggie and wiped his hands clean.

"Is that your grand gesture?" She walked to the trashcan, too. She dug around and fished out the journal. She shoved the book into William's gut.

"Keep this. It's all a man like you has."

We do our best, Maggie.

They drove in silence. Maggie had the letter that William had written for Pedro's son. He had given it to her as if it was an offering of some sort.

"Did you even know this Pedro? Or is he another person that you just listened to and decided you were a part of their life?" Maggie finally asked.

William nodded. Then he shook his head.

"What about his son?"

William took out a pen.

Never met him. Pedro spoke of him often so it feels as if I know him.

Maggie read the note.

William scribbled more.

I just listened Maggie. I looked out for you. Or that's what I thought I was doing. I'm sorry.

"I was something you stalked."

How can I make this better?

"You can't."

43

They found the house without any problem. It was small and appeared from the front to be a neat little square of a house. William looked up for a second story but there was none. Pedro had often bragged about adding on. William looked on either side of the house for the second home Pedro said he'd built but all that was there was an empty henhouse on one side and a dying lemon tree on the other. Pedro had lied.

Someone had gone to great lengths to keep the grass trim, but it was brown and frayed. The only green spot was where an old hose leaked water.

"Come on. I want to get this over with." She tugged on his arm and pulled him up toward the porch and the front door.

Maggie knocked on the door and William stood behind her. A crucifix hung ominously over the threshold of the front door and William did his best not to make eye contact with the sad gaze of Jesus Christ.

A young woman, maybe twenty-five, opened the door.

"Who are you?" she asked. Through the screen door, William could see her long black hair that she nervously twirled with her fingers.

"You don't know us, but we, well, this guy here," she said, pointing to William, "was really good friends with Pedro Mendez and he has something to give to his son Luis. Do you know where we can find him?"

But the young women hadn't heard anything after Pedro Mendez. She fell to the floor in tears. "My father," she kept saying, "*mi padrito muerto*." Finally, she got up from the floor, still weeping, and opened the screen door and let Maggie and William enter her house.

Maggie let William go in first. She was apprehensive. The weeping woman, the smallness of the living room, the lack of furniture save for a small green sofa against a back wall, the makeshift altar with candles burning the smoke of which wafted up to another crucifix and Mary, and five different pictures of the same man, gave her a feeling of cloying uneasiness.

She stared at the altar. That must be Pedro, she thought. Then she stopped. He looked vaguely familiar.

Maggie caught up with William and the woman in the kitchen. The woman had composed herself and offered beverages.

"He left when I was four. I never knew him. My younger brother Teofilo never knew him and has never seen him. Luis, my older brother, was seven.

He was always my father's favorite." The kitchen had a strawberry theme. Strawberry cookie jars, strawberry magnets, embroidered strawberries on the white curtains that framed the large kitchen window. The busyness of the kitchen seemed to make up for the sparseness of the front room.

The woman poured lemonade into three cups and passed one to Maggie and another to William, who sat around a small breakfast table. Wooden stencils of strawberry flowers adorned a vase in the center of the table.

"It's been a really tough month. I just can't believe he's gone."

Maggie couldn't make eye contact with the woman.

"I think I knew him."

"What?"

"Your dad. That was him on the mantle? His picture?" The woman nodded. Maggie looked at William.

"He used to live in our apartment complex."

William nodded.

Then the woman started crying and tried desperately to stop herself from doing just that, which only made her cry harder and longer.

Maggie looked at William to do something.

William went to her and opened the journal he hadn't let go of since Maggie had shoved it into his grasp. He showed her the entry he'd written about Luis and Pedro.

"What?" The woman asked through her sobs.

"He doesn't speak," Maggie informed her.

William put his finger over the passage he wanted her to read.

"I can't read English. My older brother Luis can but I never learned," the woman said.

Maggie grabbed the journal from William.

"Pedro is lost without Luis, his eldest son. I have heard him weeping, so strange to hear a man like Pedro weep. He cries to his girlfriend. He worries about him. He calls him a sensitive boy."

"Such beautiful words," the woman said, as she put her hand over her mouth, as if she needed to save her breath, or save the words, from escaping."Can you say them again?"

Maggie repeated the sentences.

"Are there any more?"

William nodded. He flipped through the pages and showed her other passages illuminating her father's kindness and concern for his kids, though mostly his concern was for Luis.

"Luis was his favorite," the woman said again. Maggie was intrigued by the fact this didn't seem to bother her, that the woman seemed to find some source of pride in her sibling being loved more by her father.

Maggie served as narrator. With each passage she read, the woman would clutch her heart or cry out or sit down heavier in her chair. She kept asking Maggie to read and reread.

Finally, it was time to go. Maggie handed the journal back to William. He took it from her and opened it. Then, he began to rip pages from it.

"What are you doing?' The young woman asked, hit with an instant bout of paranoia. "Why are you doing this to my father's pages?"

"Some of those pages aren't about your father," Maggie answered.

It took William fifteen minutes to shed the journal of entries other than Pedro's. When he had, he handed the journal to the young woman.

The torn pages, Maggie's pages, lay in a heap in the trashcan on top of coffee rinds and squeezed-out lemons. Maggie wanted to grab them, she wanted to save them. She wanted to give them to Jessica so she might cry and wail and realize just how much her mother loved her. But Maggie left them there, her pages, soaking in the lemon juice.

"Thank you," the woman said, as she held onto the book like a vise. "Luis is working. But, I wouldn't go there if I were you. It's not safe."

William shook his head. He was almost done with this.

"I wouldn't."

He shook his head.

"Okay," she said and directed Maggie where to drive and then gave both Maggie and William hugs before thanking them again.

They left her on the porch, examining the words she couldn't read, trying to find some hint of her father in the strange, English words.

The car idled and coughed in the otherwise silent air.

"That girl was sweet," Maggie said. "I feel bad for her."

William waited for Maggie to say more.

"I think I might stay back at Mama's a little bit longer. Just a day or two. LA isn't going anywhere. You okay with that?"

William nodded.

"Good." Maggie looked at the place where Luis worked. "This guy works in a shithole."

William looked out the window. He did.

"Okay. See you in a few." William wanted Maggie to come with him, but he knew she wouldn't. It was her leg that now shook with nerves. He let her be.

William got out of the Honda walked away from it. He walked away from Maggie but he looked back to see her as she sat behind the steering wheel, and he could see all of her. He could see in her a mime, staking a claim on a strange corner far from home, and a waitress in a diner with large orb-like eyes, foretelling the future by recalling the past. And a drug addict looking for someone stronger and stronger and stronger. He could see in her a man in jail, the Nicaraguan, in a country that hates him, dancing with ghosts.

He could see her as a fifteen year old on her first day in Los Angeles, face flushed with color, limbs jittering, as her uncle unpacked her bag from the car and told her that her new room was right over there, his short fingers pointing towards apartment 7. And then she became who she was currently, an angry woman, a lovely woman. An immigrant with two homes and two stories and two of everything that mattered. Two immigrants, he thought, alone in a car. He was like that now, too. An immigrant. He knew she would wait for him, despite her anger.

He turned and walked away from the parking lot, which was potholed and crumbling. The white lines that marked the parking spots were faded and hardly visible. He walked past the parking lot and through what once must have been a lush courtyard. It was a concrete square with benches around the edges of the concrete and trees and dead grass along the periphery behind that. In the middle of the courtyard a dry fountain stood, overwhelmed with moss and weeds. The statue in the middle of the fountain may have been a Greek bust in earlier days but was now eyeless and mouthless and noseless.

William walked through the courtyard. He wished Maggie had come with him but was glad she hadn't. Something felt off.

He entered the main building just beyond the courtyard. It had a large desk in the even-larger foyer. The desk looked like a receptionist area. An old desk chair with a broken wheel lay handicapped behind it.

He walked through the foyer and exited the back.

There were three buildings, separated from each other by courtyards similar to the one he had just walked through, in the many acres behind the foyer. The buildings made up a large compound. The size was overwhelming, more like a modern mall. William stood and stared at the three monoliths. They were painted yellow, but now

the yellow was a lazy white. On the side of one building he could read, in large red letters with a heavy font, the words: SIRE FOODS, INC.

William paused as he read the words. Sire Foods, Inc. Was he misreading?

William approached the first building, the one in the center. It was four stories, with four rows of windows stacked on top of each other. Many windows were broken. A crow danced upon a wire that shot out from the very top of the building. It squawked at something and then spread its wings and flew to it.

William entered the building. This was a building of shelves. Large, endless shelves, built from floor to ceiling, in fifteen perfect rows. They were black with silver nuts and bolts fastening them together reflecting brilliantly off the sunlight that eked in from the windows. The shelves were empty. William walked through, scanning the shelves for some clue as to what was once held there.

Food, he thought. This is where they stored food.

The building seemed empty. He reached the other end of the building, near large metal garage doors that needed a pulley system to open. He imagined a loading dock must be on the other side of the garage doors. William let his fingers run gently across the cold steel.

He left the building and walked back outside. He thought he would go and check out the building to his left. It took two minutes of walking at a steady to pace to come to it. William was sweating now, the sun relentless and strong. The only sound he heard was the screaming crow.

He entered the building. This was a building that seemed made for action. Large machinery, which seemed arcane and antiquated, something out of the last century, sat inert on the factory floor. William walked up to some sort of conveyer belt. The rubber was fraying on the sides.

"You shouldn't be here," a man's voice said from behind him.

William stopped touching the frayed rubber.

"Who are you?"

William turned to look at the speaker.

The speaker had a machine gun pointed at him. William stepped back but there was nowhere to step, so he fell over the conveyer belt. He hit his head hard on the concrete floor.

The speaker made no attempt to help him.

He pointed the gun at William with the same intense look. It was a broken look, a shard of shattered glass left behind after an accident.

William knew this was Pedro's son. He knew it because he had the same hair and the same nose, bent just to the right. William thought that had been the result of a busted nose but he now knew it was a flaw in the design.

But where Pedro was soft, Luis was dark.

"I asked what you're doing here." The words were bullets.

William shook his head.

"Do you speak Spanish?"

William nodded.

"Fucking Americans," Luis said, and shook his head back. "The factory has been closed for over a year. I'm assuming that's why you're here. We've taken it over. And do you know why? Because you assholes come down here, build this factory, use us as slaves then leave it to rot the minute you find cheaper labor in Honduras. Fuck you and fuck this factory. We've put it to better use now, old man. And if you're here to buy drugs for you or your girlfriend you can talk to the dealers just like everyone else. And if you're here as a reporter, well, I suggest you lie. We kill those people for sport. And if you're here to talk about God or repenting, well, go sell it to my mother. And if you're here for any other reason, then I don't give a fuck. Get out before someone sees you and kills you."

Luis stared at William, who didn't move.

"Do you fucking talk?"

William shook his head.

"Leave. Now." He pointed his gun and he meant it.

William searched inside his pocket. He pulled out Pedro's wooden rabbit's foot, and presented it to Luis like a gift.

William, still on the wrong side of the belt, waited for Luis to react. Luis was staring at the small, carved piece.

"My father used to carve those for me and my sister." He walked over to William and took the wooden rabbit's foot. "Yes. Just like this."

William nodded.

"He would make me climb to the top of a tree with a knife and cut down a branch big enough to carve. He gave me one for my birthday."

William nodded and smiled. Luis had put his gun down. His face softened. He seemed to forget who he was or what he was there for.

"How did you get this?"

William smiled.

"I gave it back to him when he left for the States when I was seven. That was the last time I saw the asshole."

Someone yelled Luis' name from outside.

"So you knew my father? Is that it? Or is this some cheap toy now popular in Mexico City?"

William nodded, then shook his head.

"He's dead."

William nodded.

"You came down here to give me this?"

William nodded.

"Why?"

William opened his mouth. He closed his eyes and prayed for speech.

"Well, you wasted your time. I hated him. Bastard never wrote, called, never did anything once he got to Dallas."

Luis tossed the rabbit's foot up in the air a few times, as if it were a baseball.

"If anything, this makes you less safe."

Luis threw it high towards the ceiling and shot the machine gun at it. William covered his ears. The din was deafening. Luis let more rounds fire into the air. William hid behind the conveyer belt and covered the back of his neck.

The bullets bounced off the walls of the Sire Foods building, over the oxidized steel machinery, over and over again, dancing and whirring and making new spots of decay against the flaking metal, soft as feathers now, soft as anything that was first built to endure.

"Get out of here, old man. And if I were you, I'd go out the side gate. I'm the nice one of the bunch."

William attempted to rise, but his legs didn't seem to work. And, just as his legs seemed inoperable, he felt something he had never felt before. His throat relaxed. He flexed his jaw. The entire speaking apparatus seemed whole, as though to function like this machinery once must have. It seemed ready to be used. He felt as if this was the most natural thing in the world.

"I owed him," William said. The words came out softly, a zephyr down Fountain Avenue in April. His legs still didn't work now that his voice finally did.

The words felt nice, William thought. They felt perfect in his mouth and then perfect out of his mouth.

Luis stopped, the echo of the bullets still ricocheting off the walls.

"What?"

"I owed him. That's why I came. And now I want to go somewhere quiet and rest."

It was then he felt the warmness rushing out of him but it didn't feel warm, it had the essence of warmth, of warmness, but it was neutral, it felt like nothing, really. Not pain, not panic. Just the sensation of leaving, of exodus.

"That would be nice, wouldn't it old man. Get a lady. Pull her close to you and just be quiet and rest."

"I have a woman and she has the most beautiful piece of land."

"Yeah?"

"I do. She has the most beautiful," and then William stopped.

Luis laughed. "The most beautiful what?"

William just nodded.

Luis laughed again. "You're insane."

"There's a young woman outside in a car. A Honda. Can you tell her to go on home? To just drive home, wherever that is for her, and be happy. Tell her she doesn't need me to watch over her. She never did, though I was happy to do it."

Luis didn't respond.

This is what happens to everyone and everything. He felt it now. The warmness rushing out of him. And then it wasn't warm anymore. It was wet. It was spilling out of him, the blood.

He looked at Luis, who fired another round just for the hell of it, who hadn't yet realized what happened, who hadn't yet noticed the wound in William's chest. Then William looked at the warehouse, where the bullets danced over the faded paint and the shattered windows, where the bullets would never stop shooting until the walls of Sire Foods, Inc. crumbled into nothing.

Now, with the warmness drained, he thought again of Anna, and then realized the sweet smell wasn't chili or something red, or guava or mint. It was purple, it was lavender, it was tinged with royalty and god she was beautiful, he thought. And then he sat down and whistled a melody his father had hummed, a sad melody but not too sad. For the life of him, he couldn't remember the name of the song but kept humming anyway.

AUTHOR'S ACKNOWLEDGEMENTS

This novel could never have come to being without the help of the amazing Edan Lepucki and her allies at Writer's Workshop LA, William Halfon, Luke Shanahan, Catie Disabato, Peter Hume, Millicent Rovelo, Jordana Howard, Emily Mitchell, Billy Omer Gene Stone and extra special thanks to Paul Bellaff.

Made in the USA
Columbia, SC
27 November 2017